Soul Seekers

L.D.O 'Toole

CONTENTS

ONE

❖••◦❖◦••❖

In the depths of hell, where misery and torment reigned, the devil schemed. For eons, he had tirelessly plotted and planned, searching for a way to overthrow his divine nemesis. And now, a new idea had taken hold in his infernal mind.

He had heard whispers of remarkable scientific advancements in the mortal realm. Tales of a sheep being cloned in a faraway place called Scotland had reached his ears. The mere thought of it was enough to send a shiver down his spine.

Cloning, Satan mused, could be his salvation. The scientists had created a duplicate creature from mere fragments, a feat that seemed to defy the laws of nature. If they could do that, what was stopping them from creating a clone of him, Satan himself?

The idea took hold, growing and festering in his mind like a dark seed. He could already envision the possibilities; the power that such a creation would grant him. With a clone of himself, he could rule over the mortal realm unchallenged. No one would dare stand in his way.

His thoughts churned with excitement and possibility, the flames of ambition flickered in his eyes. He would need to act quickly before anyone else thought of it and attempted to steal his idea. The devil was not known for his patience, and he was not about to let this opportunity slip away.

A rush of possibilities flooded his mind, each one more twisted and sinister than the last. With a clone, he could expand his influence exponentially, recruiting lost souls and spreading his malevolence seamlessly across the earth. No longer would he have to rely solely on his infernal minions; with two identical forms, he could be in two places at once, thus accelerating his agenda of corruption and despair.

Satan's lips curled into a wicked smile as he envisioned the chaos and destruction he could unleash upon the world. He had already perfected the technique for his demonic replacements. At the precise moment when a young, unbiased soul departed the earthly realm, a demon could slip into the vacated body. The deception was immaculate; humans could never discern the difference. Parents would accept the possessed child as their own, while the demon within subtly sowed seeds of evil.

But there was a catch - the demon soul had to be in the precise location and moment, with no angels present to interfere. Any divine intervention could potentially destroy the demon and halt the process. It was a risk that he deemed worth taking, for the potential rewards were immeasurable. If enough souls could be harvested, not only would his underground army grow, but Earth itself would eventually become overrun with demons. And then, Satan himself could walk proudly amongst them, ruling over all like a dark king on his throne. The thought sent shivers of excitement down his demonic spine.

However, Satan knew that this plan alone would not be enough to achieve his ultimate goal. He needed more - if he could be in two places at once, he could easily orchestrate his plan -he needed a vessel exactly like himself. A clone, made from every drop of darkness and malice that resided within him. Once this being was created, there would be no stopping him from conquering all that lay before him...

With a sinister smirk, Satan summoned his unholy power, conjuring a vortex of darkness that spun and churned with an otherworldly force. The black maelstrom tore through the very fabric of Hell, tunnelling through the bowels of the earth until it materialized in a scientific lab nestled in the heart of Dundee, Scotland. Three scientists, Dr. Penelope MacDonald, Professor Finley Menzies, and Professor Eligh Brown, were in the midst of their evening research when the floor beneath them began to darken and swirl like ink in water.

Penelope's eyes widened in disbelief as she witnessed the emergence of a dark swirling hole in the corner of the lab. "Holy shit," she whispered, her voice barely audible over the roar of the whirlpool. It reached its zenith, and from its churning abyss, Satan emerged.

The fallen angel towered over them, his immense form standing at a terrifying seven feet tall. His horns grazed the laboratory's ceiling, leaving deep gouges in their wake. His skin glowed with a fiery red hue, pulsating with an otherworldly energy that made the air around them feel thick and heavy. He was a monstrous hybrid of man and beast, with eyes that resembled deep pools of swirling crimson blood.

As Satan took a step forward, his presence was enough to make the scientists' knees tremble with fear and awe. The very air seemed to vibrate with his malevolent energy, causing their hearts to race with terror at the sight before them.

The sight was too much for Finley and Eligh. Overwhelmed by the sheer evilness of it all, they fainted, collapsing onto the cold, sterile floor of the lab. Penelope stood alone, her heart racing as she confronted the devil himself. Despite her middle-aged appearance, she exuded an air of confidence and intelligence, with her short, curly brown hair framing a face with compassionate brown eyes. A scientist of esteemed reputation, a Doctor with a long list of letters after her name, Penelope felt her fear rise like bile in her throat. But some primal instinct for survival kept her conscious, even as Satan's chilling presence permeated the room. Penelope gulped and steadied herself on the lab counter.

"Satan!" she gasped, her voice trembling but determined.

"Indeed," Satan growled ominously. He did not stop to make small talk- preferring to get straight to the point: "You will clone me. Now."

The command hung heavy in the air, sending chills down Penelope's spine. She knew she had no choice but to comply, even as every fibre of her rebelled against the idea. Her well-trained mind raced through a myriad of scientific protocols and procedures. With shaking hands, she began the daunting task of cloning the Prince of Darkness, manipulating sophisticated lab equipment with precision and skill.

"We'll need a sample- of your, your blood," she stammered as she faced Satan with a syringe in hand. As she initiated the sequence of drawing his blood, Finley and Eligh regained consciousness, their faces pale and bodies trembling from the shock. Despite their fear, they quickly joined Penelope in this unprecedented task, united in their determination to complete this macabre experiment.

The laboratory was awash in a dim, artificial light that seemed to sap the energy from the room. The metal tables and equipment gleamed with a cold, sterile shine. Penelope stood before Satan, the ruler of hell, her voice trembling as she explained the delicate process they would need to undertake. His piercing gaze bore down on her, his impatience palpable in the tense set of his shoulders and the creases on his brow.

"This could take some time," she began tentatively, "and we'll need to implant the embryo- umm, somewhere- for it to grow- but we don't know how long it will take for a demon baby to gestate."

"Time is a luxury you do not have," Satan growled, his deep voice rumbling with irritation.

Penelope's mind raced in a panic as she tried to think of a way to appease him. The cloning of the sheep had taken 148 days, but a human pregnancy took even longer. And with the unknown gestation period of a demon, there was no telling how long this would take. She feared what horrors the birth might bring and realized with a jolt that as the only female present, she was likely the one who would have to carry and give birth to the creature.

Satan's eyes gleamed like glowing embers as he observed her, seemingly able to read her every thought and desire. His twisted grin grew wider, revealing sharp teeth like those of a predator. He watched her mind race like a spider patiently waiting for its prey to become entangled in its web.

Desperately, she pleaded with Satan to allow them to use a sheep or cow instead, but he only responded with a derisive laugh. He saw her fear and knew that she was better suited than any animal.

"Satan," Penelope trembled, "If the implantation or birth ends up killing me...and it fails the first time...and we don't know how long it takes to grow a demon." Her voice faltered as she tried to reason with him. "I'm the only one who understands the entire procedure. It's risky, and it may not grow the first time- we had many failures before the one we called Molly grew from an embryo."

Satan's dark voice reverberated through the room as he responded to her concerns about implanting the clone within her. The sinister gleam in his eyes betrayed his amusement at her comparison to human pregnancy. "A demon--as you call my clone--will reach maturity within mere days, making the experience much faster than any human pregnancy," he retorted, seemingly having read her thoughts. A smirk played at the corners of his mouth as he added, "If there is indeed another creature capable of carrying and giving birth to my clone, then by all means, bring it forth." His piercing gaze then turned to the other scientists in the room, his tone laced with a hint of threat. "And why are you all here if she is the only one who knows the procedure? Perhaps your presence is unnecessary?" He lunged towards Eligh, and as Eligh cowered, Finley stepped forward, stumbling over his words in a desperate attempt to defend their roles on the team. Beads of sweat formed on his forehead, and his body shook with fear despite the cool temperature of the lab. It was clear that Satan's power and presence alone instilled terror in those around him. Satan grinned and stepped back, resuming his pacing as he kept a constant watch on the three scientists.

Eligh, seizing the opportunity, called through to another lab, emphasizing the top-secret nature of their project. After a brief conversation, he arranged for a young ewe to be delivered. Fifteen minutes later, the familiar 'baa' from outside signalled its arrival. The ewe, adorned with a collar and lead, was brought inside by Eligh.

During the implantation procedure, an unforeseeable catastrophe struck. A large mirror on the laboratory wall shattered as Satan peered into it, shattering it into thousands of fragments, sending shards hurtling across the room like deadly projectiles. One particularly jagged piece landed in the cloning apparatus, mingling with Satan's extracted DNA. No one dared interrupt the chaos, not with the devil himself watching so intently.

Finley and Eligh assisted Penelope in carefully implanting the embryo into the ewe's uterus. Their hands shook with nerves, and sweat dripped from their brows.

Under Satan's relentless scrutiny, they witnessed the embryo's alarming growth over the next 14 agonizing days. On the fourteenth day, the ewe—whom they had named Mary—gave birth- if you can call it that- to a monstrosity. The delivery was gruesome; the creature clawed its way out of Mary's body, leaving her in tatters. Blood streamed from the poor animal as the beast, with its fully formed horns and hooves, emerged, a grotesque blend of human and beast. Penelope, Finley, and Eligh watched in pure horror as the nightmare unfolded before their eyes.

The creature's growth was a terrifying sight. Its body expanded at an alarming rate, its limbs stretching and contorting until it stood as tall as a toddler in just a few short hours. By the seventy-second hour, it had reached its full size, towering over the exhausted and fearful scientists like a true devil incarnate.

As the process came to an end, a perfect doppelgänger of Satan emerged, stepping out from the shadows. It was an eerie mirror image, every horrifying detail perfectly replicated. The clone possessed the same twisted grin as Satan himself, scars and bruises marring its face just like its creator's. This being radiated with raw power and dark energy, destined to spread evil and destruction on earth just as efficiently as Satan.

Satan gazed upon his creation with a sense of pride and satisfaction. This was his ultimate masterpiece, his answer to subjugating all of humanity. He could feel the immense power pulsating through this clone, ready to do his bidding without hesitation.

"He is perfect," Satan declared with a voice that boomed like thunder. "Although born more as a reflection than a true clone, it matters not." He turned to the scientists behind him, his eyes gleaming with malice. "Now," he intoned, "it begins."

Penelope, Finley, and Eligh exchanged horrified glances, realizing too late the grave mistake they had made by creating this abomination. But what else could they have done? For if they had refused Satan, surely they would all be dead. They could only watch in terror as Satan's plan came to fruition before their very eyes.

At that moment, a terrible realization settled in their minds like a shroud - the earth would soon face its darkest days yet.

Satan and his clone stood in the centre of the ravaged lab, their twin forms casting menacing shadows on the walls. The air crackled with residual energy from their dark ritual. The scientists huddled together, their faces pale and eyes wide with fear but still very much alive. Mary the sheep lay dead in a pool of blood- her eyes not seeing the horror she had brought into this world.

Satan turned his piercing gaze towards them, a cruel smile curling on his lips. "Your lives have been spared, for now. You have served your purpose," his voice echoed, each word dripping with malevolent intent. "But remember this: what you have witnessed here must never be spoken of. Tell a soul, and your fate will be worse than death." He leaned in closer, his red eyes blazing with power. "And if needed, I will return for more clones - and you will serve me."

The three scientists nodded vigorously, their fear palpable. They had seen enough to understand the gravity of their situation and did not need further convincing. The shadows deepened as Satan's clone stepped forth, ready to fulfil its unholy purpose under the command of its nefarious creator.

With a final malevolent glare at the scientists, Satan beckoned to his clone. "I shall name thee 'Natas' - Come- Brother," he commanded.

Together, they stepped toward the swirling vortex that still hung menacingly in the room, an open passage back to the underworld.

As they entered the abyss and the hole closed over behind them, a sudden gust of icy wind swept through the lab, extinguishing all sources of light and leaving the room shrouded in darkness. The

scientists clung to each other, their trembling bodies the only movement in the oppressive silence that followed.

Satan and his clone descended through the churning vortex, the underworld's familiar heat and darkness welcoming them. As they emerged on the other side, the landscape of Hell unfurled before them—an endless expanse of fire-lit caverns and sulphurous pits echoing with the agonized wails of the damned.

In the darkest depths of hell, where flames licked at the tortured souls and screams echoed endlessly, there were a select few who shone with an otherworldly brilliance.

Despite the fact that Natas was Satan's identical clone, possessing the same memories and intense animosity, Satan still felt compelled to provide an explanation-

These were the stolen children, taken by demons at their last gasp of life before the angels could claim them.

It would take a precise twenty years for their radiance to diminish and finally plunge into an abyss of darkness. But once this transformation occurred on the exact twentieth anniversary, they would be transformed into the most obedient and reliable followers in all of hell, serving as Satan's faithful army. In this moment, these golden souls roamed freely throughout the fiery landscape, their radiant forms casting a haunting aura upon the desolate terrain.

As each new child was brought down to hell, they were fiercely guarded by hulking demons with eyes of fire. Their massive claws gleamed in the dim light as they stood watch over the fragile, innocent souls. They knew the stakes - if this child were to be somehow revived in the earthly realm, their hold on its soul would be broken, and it would return to its origin, lost forever in the light. And if the child's earthly body had been inhabited by a demon, the consequences would be even more dire - the demon would be cast out and obliggerated or forced to return to hell. The air was thick with tension as they waited for the final decision - would this precious golden soul remain in their grasp or be snatched back into the light, escaping their clutches once and for all? The fiery glow of their eyes intensified with anticipation as they braced themselves for the outcome. Once a full day had passed without a word from above, the demons loosened their grip and allowed the golden souls to roam freely within the depths of hell. They did so with caution, knowing that they would never again return to their earthly bodies or realm. But still, there was a glimmer of hope within these golden souls - a chance that one day they may break free from their demonic possession and return to the light. As time passed, their glowing forms slowly dimmed until, eventually, they forgot all about their former lives and surrendered completely to serving Satan for eternity.

Natas surveyed his surroundings, taking in the endless expanse of fire and brimstone. Passing by a few of the golden souls who had been living in hell for a while but not long enough yet for their shine to dim, Satan reiterated to his clone the significance of these rare beings in their realm - how they were coveted and protected at all costs.

Satan led the way to his command centre, a massive fortress carved into the black rock at the heart of Hell. As they entered, lesser demons scattered, recognizing the unimaginable power now walking among them. They reached the war room, a cavernous hall lined with maps and dark artifacts, where Satan's generals and advisors awaited.

"Brothers, behold," Satan declared, his voice booming through the chamber. "Our hopes for dominion over the earthly realm have been renewed. My clone, a perfect reflection of my darkest essence, now stands among us."

The demon generals, grotesque and fearsome creatures, bowed deeply in acknowledgment. They could sense the tremendous power emanating from the clone and knew it would play a pivotal role in their future plans.

Satan turned to his clone, gesturing to the schematics and vision pool spread across the vast stone table in the centre of the hall. "We begin anew- The humans have no idea what we've unleashed. With you sharing my burden, we will enact our plan swifter than ever imagined."

Together, they poured over the maps of the earthly realm, marking territories ripe for corruption and souls susceptible to temptation. The plan was expansive: covertly embedding demons into positions of power, manipulating leaders, and igniting conflicts that would lead to chaos and despair. The chosen demons would report to Satan.

Satan smiled wickedly, his voice low as he shared his plans with his clone. "I have already begun my work," he announced, a hint of malice in his eyes. "Politics, religion, and war have always been my tools for spreading chaos and discord. For many years, I have been plotting and planning, quietly infiltrating the upper echelons of human society. My power will remain hidden, undetected by even the most vigilant of enemies. And once my plans come to fruition, they will be unstoppable." His maniacal laughter echoed throughout the grand chamber, bouncing off the ornate walls and ceiling as he continued his sinister speech.

"And now, with your help, my brother, we can begin to take over the earth one soul at a time. You will be in charge of my newest project - manipulating and corrupting the golden souls, replacing them with demons through our new church. And the best part? The humans will bring their innocent children to us willingly." As the flames flickered around him, Satan's plans for world domination that had seemed so far off just over two weeks ago seemed within reach.

The clone nodded, absorbing every aspect of the plan, calculating the most efficient ways to sow destruction. "And the scientists? " he inquired, his voice identical to Satan's own but tinged with a hint of curiosity. "I can go back and kill them," he offered, already turning away, but Satan stopped him- "They may be useful again in the future should we require more clones," he replied with a sinister chuckle. "Their silence is assured by their fear. They will continue their work, oblivious to the darkness they've helped unleash until the time comes when they are no longer useful."

Days turned into weeks as Satan and his clone tirelessly refined their strategies, summoning demonic legions and crafting intricate webs of deceit. Their infernal synergy was unparalleled; where one left off, the other began an unending cycle of malevolence.

On the surface, the world remained blissfully ignorant of the cataclysmic force being marshalled against it. Life continued in its ordinary rhythm, unaware that the very fabric of reality was being meticulously unravelled by two avatars of evil hidden in the shadows.

But for those in the know, the air seemed to grow colder and the nights darker, as though the world itself sensed an impending doom it could not yet comprehend. The gears of the apocalypse had been set in motion, guided by the hand of Satan and his perfect reflection.

And so, Hell prepared to make its mark upon the Earth, one wicked plot at a time.

Satan's eyes glowed with satisfaction as he surveyed the demonic map, a meticulous diagram of earthly influence and dark intent. His clone, Natas, stood beside him, indistinguishable in form and power, ready to execute the next phase of their insidious plan.

Satan's gaze was fixed upon a vision pool showing a young man who had been a source of great fascination for the dark lord since his birth.

From the moment of his birth, this human had been marked by darkness. In a moment of brief death, a powerful demon had taken possession of his body, refusing to relinquish control even when the human was resurrected. Such rare and potent feats intrigued Satan. The human's eyes now held an otherworldly glow, his movements slightly distorted as if being pulled by invisible strings. Despite his possession, there remained a distinctly human element to him - a longing for love that had yet to be satisfied. However, he maintained control over the demon within him, exerting his own thoughts and will at his whim. He even commanded other demons to do his bidding, making him the ultimate embodiment of evil - something that deeply piqued Satan's interest. For some time, Satan had believed that this exceptional mortal did not belong in the earthly realm, and now it seemed the time had come for him to be put to use by the dark lord. With intense focus, Satan observed as the pieces fell into place for his plan involving this enigmatic individual.

"It's time," Satan declared, his voice a deep rumble that echoed throughout the war room. "Descend to the human world. Take on a human form so you don't frighten anyone, but remember the human form will only last 24 hours; after that, you will need to return to the underworld if you have not completed your mission, but never lose sight of our goal."

Natas nodded, understanding his mission with a clarity only an incarnation of Satan could possess. With a twisted smile on his blackened lips and a glint of madness in his eyes, the dark figure declared, "I will build an empire of devoted followers as we have planned".

Satan pointed to the vision pool displaying Nicholas Green meticulously tying a noose, "Start with this one," he directed.

"I have been watching this one. He is perfect for the mission. "Natas nodded his approval as he stepped into the portal that would transport him to the human realm, his form shifting and morphing until he appeared as a strikingly handsome young man with sharp features, curly dark hair and eyes that glowed red in the darkness.

He appeared on Earth in an explosion of rocks and dirt, materializing in the poorly lit basement of Nicholas Green's apartment building. As his body solidified, glowing red eyes blinked open, the only remnants of his demonic origin. The space around him was musty and damp, with shadows creeping along the walls like eerie fingers. The air was thick with the stench of decay and evil, and he revelled in it. This was his domain now. He brushed the dust from his pants and found his way to Nicholas Green's apartment.

TWO

Nicholas Green slammed the front door shut with a forceful kick. He flung the crumpled piece of paper in his hand to the floor and made his way through the cramped kitchen into his bedroom. He sank heavily onto the edge of his unmade single bed and reached underneath, pulling out a long, thick piece of twine. He grasped it tightly in his calloused hands, scrutinizing it as if seeing it for the first time. Of course, it wasn't- he had played with that piece of twine for years, perfecting a hangman's noose whenever he felt despondent, only to unravel it and stash it back under the bed. But this time was not the same. For the first time in his young life, he was serious.

Suicide seemed like the only escape from the wretched existence he called his life.

The thought had crossed his mind many times before, but today was different. Today, he was utterly defeated.

Despite all his hard work, he had absolutely nothing to show for it: no career, no money, and no Shelley by his side. The thought of her made him sad and then angry.

He had always prided himself on his intelligence, believing that once he graduated from university, everything would fall effortlessly into place - including winning the heart of Shelley. But she seemed oblivious to him, not even acknowledging his existence. He had been enamoured with her from afar for years, admiring the way her golden hair shone in the sunlight and how her laughter filled the air like music. He had been convinced that she would eventually be his. His plan was to land a prestigious job at one of the top law firms in New York, combined with his good looks to win her over. But now, on top of everything else, he was facing eviction.

At nearly 24 years old, he felt far older. Rejection had become a constant companion - from potential employers, now his apartment, and from the love of his life. He was drained, exhausted, utterly spent, and officially a loser- as predicted by his contemptuous parents. It seemed as if the world had forced him to his knees and kicked him directly in the gut- Hard.

As his fingers absentmindedly worked the twine, he closed his eyes and let his mind retrace the sorrowful journey of his life.

His first memory played out like an out-of-body experience, with shadows clawing at him from every direction like a recurring nightmare.

He saw a newborn baby struggling for its first breath, its airway obstructed. The young midwife held the lifeless infant, legs tucked under one arm, head cradled, two fingers scooping out the gunk blocking his throat. Darkness surrounded him until he finally drew his first breath and opened his eyes, scattering the shadows.

The baby was silent except for the steady rhythm of his breathing. The shadows hovered around the room, closing in on his mother. Baby Nicholas watched wide-eyed as the midwife placed him in an incubator and turned back to the woman lying still on the hospital bed. A nurse shouted, and the room quickly filled with noise and personnel—doctors, nurses, and the life-saving midwife crowded around the blood-soaked bed.

Nicholas couldn't look away; he knew instinctively that his mother was dying. The shadows now engulfed her as a bright light rose from the bed. He instinctively understood it was her soul, floating gently towards the ceiling.

The room was a sea of swirling dark shadows, fiercely reaching out for the glimmer of light. It was a constant struggle as they clawed at her, attempting to pull her down while she desperately tried to float upwards.

The blood dripped noisily onto the floor, and the machines emitted a continuous, thin beep.

Doctors and nurses obscured his view of her lifeless body. He could only hear the frantic shouts from the doctor: "Clear!" and everyone stepped back. Again, the same voice commanded, "Clear!"

Finally, her soul floated back down to the bed and was gone- back inside her, as if it was being pulled back by some invisible strings- the shadows still clawing madly at her subsided. The machine started to emit a steady beep, beep, beep—she had been saved. And the shadows danced around the room in an angry dance.

In all the excitement, Nicholas realized he had been holding his breath or something was blocking his airway. Now, as he tried to suck in some air, he found himself gasping silently, his tiny body writhing. And then, it all just stopped. He ceased his struggle and, at that moment, noticed the shadows had turned their full focus on him. To them, capturing a 'perfect soul' like his was the ultimate prize. They may have lost the mother, but now they sought to claim him.

As his soul began to drift away from his body, floating effortlessly upwards, a powerful demon saw its chance and entered his tiny body.

The same young midwife who had earlier placed baby Nicholas in the incubator noticed the baby had stopped breathing and shouted, drawing everyone's attention. The horde of Doctors and Nurses now turned to him- crowding around him as the doctor started CPR. Within minutes, his soul returned swiftly to his small body. Nicholas drew a breath, filling it with life once more. His body and mind felt crowded now, unlike the calmness he experienced when he took his first breath. Chaos was in his head, yet his breathing was steady, and his heartbeat was strong. He closed his eyes and slept.

Three of the shadows —demons— that had tried to pull his soul down to the depths of hell remained with him every day of his grim existence, surrounding him constantly. He watched as they danced on the walls and the ceilings in his every waking moment. The fourth, the one that shared his body- that lived within him, incessantly chattered to him. As a result, he never cried as a baby and was never alone.

He learned to communicate with the dancing demons through his thoughts, as if by magic. They always responded and acted on his desires. They never left him entirely; at least one demon always stayed close. As a baby, whenever he thought of food and it wasn't being provided, the demons would bring his mother to him. At first, she didn't understand what was happening. The first few times, she struggled, but the demons would push and drag her by any means necessary until she found herself standing at her son's crib, intuitively knowing what he needed. The whispers in her head were not from her son but from the demons, manipulating her to fulfill his unspoken desires. Soon, she stopped resisting the demons and came willingly whenever she heard the voices and felt their pull. She would never admit this to anyone, especially not to Nicholas's father, but she was terrified of this baby and the immense power he seemed to have over her. She couldn't tell anyone; how could she without them thinking she had lost her mind? So, she did what the baby wanted and left him alone the rest of the time.

After a few days in the hospital, they brought him home, where he spent most days lying in his crib in the cramped living room, with no stimulation except from the demons. He was bottle-fed just enough to keep him alive, the bottle propped up on a pillow. If his mother held him for too long after changing his soiled diaper, his father would yell at her. His father was consumed by a deep, burning jealousy whenever his wife turned her attention towards their newborn. In his mind, he alone deserved her love and adoration. She was always eager to please her man and would often put her son on the back burner as she indulged in drugs or alcohol- After all, the father was the provider.

On rare occasions, when the old man went out, she would sometimes hold Nicholas for a short while. Those moments were few and far between. However, there was no love or affection in those moments; it was as if she were holding him to figure out how this little person could possibly be controlling her, leaving Nicholas to find solace only in the presence of the demons that hovered close- they filled the void of parental affection and interaction. If it weren't for the demons, Nicholas might never have learned to walk or talk. At the very least, he would have been a very slow developer. But the demons taught him everything he would ever need to know.

Thanks to the demons, Nicholas learned quickly and efficiently, far surpassing what his neglectful parents could offer him in terms of development and education. From an early age, he harboured a deep resentment towards them, understanding all too well the dysfunctional dynamic of his family and the ways in which they failed him.

They could barely afford their small rental apartment in Fordham—one of the cheapest and roughest neighbourhoods in the Bronx—but they always seemed to find enough money for booze, weed, and cigarettes— the essentials. Some weeks, they lived on stolen vegetables from the neighbours' rooftop garden. There was no meat, no milk, just steamed vegetables and vegetable broth, which his mother called soup. Ugh, soggy vegetables. The thought made his stomach churn. For the first time in years, Nick allowed his mind to wander even further into his past.

Although he had shown from a very early age that he was smarter than most children his age, neither of his parents had encouraged him to pursue any further studies beyond the mandatory. In fact, they had done just the opposite.

Then there was his baby sister, Shammawana. Even at the age of seven, Nick had thought her name was ridiculous. "What were they thinking?" he often wondered. "They must have been on some serious drugs when they named her."

"Shammawana" wasn't even a real name. It was ridiculous. That's what it was.

Despite his aversion to his parents, Nick felt a peculiar mixture of disdain and reluctant sorrow toward his sister. She, too, was a victim of their parents' neglect and poor choices. Yet, even though he thought her name was stupid, he couldn't entirely dismiss the responsibility he felt for her. She was, after all, part of the same dysfunctional family that had trapped him in a life he despised.

The sinister voice in his mind had been urging him to take her life since the day she arrived home, and even without its influence, he knew he would have done the same- eventually. That infant had brought nothing but chaos. Her constant wails grated on his nerves, and he was weary of attempting to silence her. His parents, always quick to scold him for her cries, only added to his frustration. They were unfit to raise a child, he thought bitterly. On the night of her demise, when Shamawana was only 12 weeks old, the malevolent voice echoed relentlessly in his head, whispering, "End her, suffocate her, end her…suffocate her." The three dark entities revelled in anticipation, dancing delightedly on the walls and ceiling as he clutched her tightly, pressing her delicate face against his chest to stifle her breath. Gradually, her struggles ceased, and he witnessed the radiant glow of her soul departing her body. Two of the shadows eagerly reached out to claim her soul as they floated upwards, pulling her down through the floorboards into an unknown abyss. The third shadow missed his opportunity to seize her body. It momentarily ceased its dance, standing still as it watched the others pull her essence down. Nicholas gently lay her lifeless form back in her crib. He covered her with a soft blanket before retiring to his own bed.

As he closed his eyes, all three shadows returned and resumed their eerie dance upon his walls.

His parents came under investigation, but the coroner's verdict attributed her death to sudden infant death syndrome. He pushed the memories of her demise to the darkest corners of his mind, never wanting to revisit them until this moment. The family maintained a solemn silence regarding her from the day she was buried - as if she had never existed.

During his school days, Nick had a solitary 'friend' named Chuck, a diminutive boy who was often the target of ridicule due to his small stature, thick glasses, and reserved nature. Nick paid little attention to the taunts directed at Chuck. He was just grateful that they diverted the teasing away from him. Despite their initial limited interactions, they were frequently seated together by teachers and gradually formed a bond, spending their recess and lunch breaks in each other's company. This companionship, born out of circumstance, began at the tender age of five and endured as a source of comfort for both boys. However, their friendship took a drastic turn when Chuck made the ill-fated mistake of laughing at Nick when they were nine years old. It was a day etched in Nick's memory - as they sat together in the schoolyard during lunch, they watched the other children kicking a ball around in an impromptu game of football. Chuck sat with tears welling in his eyes and such a sad look on his face as he told Nick how he wanted 'so badly' to be a part of the group, and Nick felt a twinge of sympathy for his 'friend', something rare for him. In a moment of raw emotion, Nick began to open up to Chuck about the shadows that seemed to follow him everywhere and was about to tell him about the menacing voice that constantly whispered in his head- but before he could continue, Chuck burst out laughing, causing Nick to stop in his tracks and abandon his confession.

As Nick closed up about his unsettling experiences, Chuck's uncontrollable laughter drew the attention of their peers in the play area. "We all have shadows, Nick," Chuck managed to utter amidst fits of hysterical laughter. Nick's anger simmered beneath the surface, fuelled by the mocking response from his friend and the sinister whispers in his mind. Silently he vowed to 'Snuff Chuck', a chilling determination settled within him as he smirked at the wittiness of his dark thought before walking away.

As the school day drew to a close, Nick's resolve solidified, and he silently gave the order. Two shadowy figures, unseen by the onlookers, eagerly danced towards Chuck as he made his way to the stairwell. With one on each side, they propelled him over the railing, his expression frozen in a silent scream of shock as he plummeted towards the unforgiving concrete below. To the witnesses, it appeared as if Chuck had tripped and tragically fallen from the second-floor stairwell. The shadows concealed their sinister role in the fatal incident. Nick trailed behind Chuck with just enough distance to avoid suspicion but close enough to catch every detail. He replayed the scene in his mind, relishing in the moment over and over. Each time, a surge of triumph and satisfaction coursed through him like electricity.

Following the tragic accident, Chuck never regained consciousness and succumbed to his injuries the next day in the hospital. Nick was questioned by the authorities as a witness, and the police investigation concluded that it was a horrific accident.

The news of Chuck's tragic death spread like wildfire through the school, igniting an outpouring of sympathy from his peers. Nick was flooded with countless condolences and well-wishes, but no one could see the twisted emotions brewing beneath his facade of grief. As he struggled to contain a sick sense of pleasure over Chuck's demise, he confided in Katie Studson, when she approached him as he sat alone in the playground; she was a little younger than Nick and was one of the popular girls at school, Nick wanted nothing more than to see her reaction. He felt a sense of satisfaction as he revealed to her that he was actually glad his former friend had died- adding that maybe he had had something to do with it.

Much to his pleasure, Katie's face contorted in horror as she listened to his shocking confession. Without a word, she turned and ran off to tell others about his callousness. But before she could get far, Nick called out to her, "You'll be next if you go telling on me!" His words sent a chill down her spine, and she stopped dead in her tracks.

She turned back to look at Nick with a mixture of fear and anger on her face and then quickly resumed her escape- determined to expose him to the rest of the school. But as she ran frantically through the playground, trying to reach safety, Nick summoned his shadows, dark and menacing, to take action against her. With a sudden burst of energy, they surged forward like a pack of wolves, surrounding her on all sides. A loud crack echoed through the air as they shoved her with brutal force onto the unforgiving cement path. The impact was jarring and violent, resulting in a broken jaw, shattered teeth, and a sharp pain pulsing through her left wrist.

After her accident, an ambulance was called to transport Katie to the hospital. The school brushed it off as a simple accident, but she knew the real reason behind it: Nick. She tried to explain to everyone that it was Nick who caused the accident, but no one believed her because he was too far away at the time.

Despite her unfortunate encounter with Nick, Katie refused to stay silent about his dark statement. When she returned to school Nick calmly threatened her to keep her mouth shut or risk ending up like Chuck. From that point on, people were hesitant around Nick, unsure if what Katie had said was true or rumour. Until this moment, he had buried his memories of Chuck and Katie deep within his mind, never feeling a need to revisit them.

When he was about 12 years old, he came home from school one day to find the apartment filled with smoke; that in itself was not unusual, but this time, it was smokier because there were more people. Five people, including his parents, were sitting around the kitchen table, drinking cheap wine and smoking weed from a grimy-looking bong. The ashtray overflowed with cigarette butts, and some of the butts still smouldered. The air was thick with the pungent odour of smoke and burnt herbs. He weaved through the tight kitchen, making his way towards his bedroom. The women, including his mother, were fawning over him and laughing drunkenly about what a big boy he was now, and his father tried to involve him in the smoking session; it was the closest thing his father had ever done to encourage him in any way.   At first, he was flattered by the offer, but as the scent of weed and cigarettes washed over him, his stomach turned. He declined, saying that he didn't like the smell, which caused a flash of anger to cross his father's face.

"You think you're better than us, don't you, boy? Well, I've got news for you – you're not. You'll be drinking soon enough and looking at me to get you drugs too, probably, and maybe then we'll have something to talk about," his father said, giving him a shove as he tried to leave. Nick retreated to his room and stayed there until the session was over and everyone had either passed out or left.

As he transitioned to high school, he struggled to contain the fiery rage that simmered within him. He knew that if anyone found out about his involvement in his friend's death, he could face serious consequences. The fear of being locked up consumed him, but despite his efforts to control himself, there were moments when caution slipped from his grasp. When he let his guard down in those fleeting lapses, two of his teachers met their untimely fates.

The first incident occurred during his freshman year when his science teacher, Mr Lawson, suffered a fatal mishap that resulted in the loss of his face during a classroom experiment. He had been demonstrating how different liquids can affect the way paper burns when the Bunsen burner used in the experiment exploded, sending flames spouting upwards; the teacher's hair and face went up in flames like dry grass in a paddock. Horrified students flocked to extinguish the flames, but despite their heroics, he died before any medical attention was received. Paramedics cited he had suffered a fatal heart attack because of the burns and possibly the shock of it all.

Nick remained calmly seated, unmoved by the chaos unfolding around him. His face was a mask of impassive calm, but inwardly he felt a sense of satisfaction at the spectacle before him. The wild frenzy of emotions and actions played out like a well-choreographed dance that he found extremely entertaining to witness.

The smell of burning flesh and hair was intense, and he realised he had a favourite method for killing now. It was noted that Mr Lawson had just confronted Nick about his careless handling of a Bunsen burner minutes before the tragedy, publicly embarrassing him in front of the entire class.

All eyes in the classroom turned to Nick, the air thick with suspicion and accusation. The students exchanged knowing glances while the teachers furrowed their brows, searching for any sign of guilt on Nick's face. But he remained cool and collected, knowing that all it would take was a few words from him, and his demons would dance to do his bidding. As evidence, they confiscated the Bunsen burner that had caused Mr. Lawson's tragic death. However, after a thorough investigation, the police concluded that it was merely an unfortunate accident. Despite this, the whispers and sideways glances towards Nick continued as if the lingering scent of suspicion could never truly be washed away.

Tragedy struck again the following year when Mr. Jonas, Nick's physical education teacher, was fatally impaled by a javelin in the sports shed. The grisly discovery was made by another student who had gone to return the equipment at the end of the day. Earlier that day, Mr. Jonas had scolded Nick in front of the class for mishandling a javelin, which ultimately led to his death. Regardless of Nick's absence from the sports shed and lack of direct evidence linking him to the incident, suspicions arose among faculty and students about his involvement. The police investigation could not find any solid connection to Nick, and the death was once again ruled as an unfortunate accident by the coroner. Despite the lack of concrete evidence- whispers and hushed conversations about him being either cursed or dangerous spread like wildfire, igniting fear and suspicion throughout the halls. Students and teachers alike avoided any unnecessary contact with Nicholas Green for fear of becoming the next victim of an unfortunate "accident." The air itself seemed to hold its breath, waiting for the next tragedy to strike at any moment.

Secretly, he was happy to be left alone; he preferred his own company anyway (and that of the demons).

From the moment he was old enough to work, his father constantly yelled at him to "just get a bloody job!" He would say, "You're not meant to be some college boy; you're a working boy, just like us.

Where in hell do you think you're going to get money for college, hey boy? Get it out of your head that you're going to be somebody — you are not. You were born a Green, and you'll die a Green. You're nothing but a piece of shit."

Every time his father would start on him, Nick would stand looking at his feet until the rant was over. He never intended to go to college anyway—university, yes, but not college—and so he would agree with the old man to avoid further conflict.

"Would it kill you to help support your family, Nicky?" his mother's words, though gentler, held the same dismissive meaning. Nick hated being called Nicky; she only used it when she wanted something from him, which irritated him even more.

Nick's contempt for his parents turned into a grim determination. He would break free from the destiny they tried to impose upon him. He would become something more, something powerful, and something that went beyond the narrow scope of their lives. The demons had seen to that, and Nick was ready to embrace whatever it took to leave his unfortunate beginnings far behind.

At the age of fourteen (and much to the demons' delight), Nick concluded that the only way out of his embarrassing and infuriating family situation was for both his parents to die. Over the years, the demon in his head had thoughtfully devised numerous scenarios to fulfil Nick's dark wishes—but Nick was intelligent. That accident would have to wait; he couldn't risk the drama of being placed with a foster family or, worse, being put in a home while finishing his schooling.

To keep his parents off his back, he diligently took on a part-time job at the local market. Stacking shelves three nights a week after school and every Saturday, then dutifully handed his pay check over to his mother every month.

The demon's whispers were like a sinister, persistent voice, constantly tempting and goading Nick to give in to his darker impulses, and it seemed like accidents were constantly occurring in his presence. Everyone around him was cautious and even wary of him - from his coworkers to his employers. The rumours from high school had followed him everywhere, and the frequent incidents at the market only added more weight to them.

When he wasn't working or studying, he channelled his boundless energy into physical pursuits. Every day at 5 am, like clockwork, he would jog through the streets with a fierce determination, his muscles burning and sweat dripping down his face. And when he wasn't out pounding the pavement, he could be found hoisting weights in the school gym, grunting and straining as he pushed his body to its limits. Even during lunch breaks and precious moments of free time at school, he couldn't resist the call of physical activity. It was like a fire burning inside him that could only be quenched by movement and exertion.

His newfound passion developed into an all-consuming fixation, and by the end of high school, he had completely transformed himself; he stood at an impressive height of six foot two, towering over most of his peers. He was muscular and lean, and his sharp jawline and chiselled features gave him a ruggedly handsome appearance.

As he turned eighteen and completed his senior year with top Honors, his exceptional academic achievements amassed praise from his teachers, who momentarily set aside their apprehensions about him to celebrate his success at the graduation ceremony. Nick's outstanding performance set him apart in a school where few students reached their senior year, let alone excelled in every subject. However, his parents were notably absent from the event, with his father dismissing it as a waste of time.

Unbeknownst to his parents, Nick secretly applied to and was accepted into the prestigious Columbia University to pursue a degree in law. Securing a small government grant to support his studies, Nick's future seemed promising. Upon receiving the confirmation email, he issued a chilling command to the malevolent forces that lingered around him, instructing them to eliminate his parents with a single directive - "burn them." A devastating fire ensued, tragically claiming the lives of not only his parents but also thirty-eight other innocent residents in the apartment complex.

In Nick's twisted perspective, the fire that claimed the lives of his parents and thirty-eight others was a twisted act of fate that he viewed as a favour to the world. He harboured a deep-seated disdain for the residents of the building, believing them to be insignificant and undeserving of life. To Nick, they were just a bunch of self-absorbed oxygen-wasters, leeching off the world's resources without a care. He cursed them under his breath, fuck them all, he thought- he hoped they all rotted in hell. He only wished he could have been there to see it and smell it. Despite his callous thoughts, the authorities sympathized with him, viewing him as a victim who had tragically lost both parents in the blaze. Nick's alibi of being at work during the fire and his adept ability to feign emotions like a seasoned actor shielded him from suspicion.

The police investigation concluded that the fire was not suspicious, attributing its cause to a candle left burning in his parent's living room while they were asleep, likely under the influence of alcohol or drugs. Nick's calculated performance as the grieving son earned him the sympathy and support of those around him, masking his true intentions with a facade of grief and trauma. His skilful portrayal of emotions hinted at a hidden talent for acting, a path he might have pursued if not for his interest in law.

Throughout his three years at the University, Nick maintained a solitary existence, keeping to himself and concealing the darkness that lurked within him.

He had emerged into a sea of unfamiliar faces, each one overlapping with the next. The overwhelming noise of chatter and laughter filled the university halls, but Nick kept his distance. He observed them from afar, considering them as mere acquaintances rather than potential friends. Despite being surrounded by a horde of peers, he felt a sense of isolation in this new environment.

Balancing his studies with a part-time job at the market, he limited his work hours to one evening a week and either a Saturday or Sunday afternoon.

Despite his striking features, Nick's appearance seemed to do little to boost his standing or popularity among his peers. Lingering rumours from high school cast a shadow of caution around him, causing students and lecturers to keep their distance. His dorm mates - Tommy Perkins, Shane O'Donahue, and Eddie Sampson - had formed a tight-knit group since their school years, embracing the university experience with a focus on revelry and socializing. They arrived at uni as expected from their privileged backgrounds, but their main goal was to indulge in partying and getting laid. Initially, they tried to include Nick in their social activities, extending invitations to parties. However, when he responded, it was with cold glares and minimal engagement. Their attempts at humour would often devolve into mean-spirited jabs at Nick's social skills, even going so far as to speculate about him having Asperger's syndrome. Despite their attempts to undermine him, Nick remained unfazed. The three constantly played pranks on Nick - hiding his belongings and laughing as he frantically searched for them, purposely messing up his meticulously arranged books and papers, and slyly moving his laptop and phone when he wasn't looking.

The dorm mates thought they were being humorous by sending notes signed with Nick's name to the attractive girls in their classes. He always knew because the girls would look over at him when they were reading the notes and giggle. The foolishness of their actions was apparent to Nick, but he brushed it off for the most part. However, his focus shifted just months before Uni was finished when they targeted the one girl he had his sights set on - Shelley Knights.

Throughout his university years, no other classmate had captivated Nick's attention like the alluring Shelley Knights. Her intelligence shone in every lecture; her popularity was evident by the swarm of friends that always surrounded her. With striking features and a kind demeanour, Shelley stood out among her peers. Nick decided after University he would pursue her- best to wait until he was a successful lawyer, and then she would not be able to say no; she would find him irresistible with all his money and success; he already had the looks- he knew. For now, he just smiled when he saw her, and she always smiled demurely back. Shelley was one of the few who didn't live on campus, so not long after he met her, he discreetly followed her one afternoon as she walked home. She lived in a nice house with a big yard and secure fencing- an obvious sign of a wealthy family. Sometimes at night, he would watch her through his binoculars from the bushes opposite her house. That's how he knew so much about her. He saw her through the sheer curtains of her room on the hot evenings as she undressed. Little. Miss. Perfect- He would smile as he watched her, and sometimes he would slide his free hand inside his pants and stroke himself while he watched.

When she received the note purportedly from Nick, she simply smiled at him with genuine kindness, tucking the note into her book bag. Though it was a gentle rejection, it fuelled Nick's desire for her even more.

He stormed back to his dorm room, anger boiling inside of him- How dare they try to ridicule him in front of Shelley? He seethed with a fiery intensity, waiting for one of them, or all of them, to come back so he could confront them. The air in the room was thick with tension and raw emotion as he paced back and forth, thoughts of revenge consuming his mind.

When Eddie finally returned- alone, he couldn't contain his rage any longer. With a dangerous look in his eyes, he set his demons on Eddie, who was completely caught off guard. In an instant, two shadowy figures appeared and hoisted him high into the air. Nick went over and lounged on his bed with a wicked grin on his face, watching as they held him suspended.

"I warned you to leave me alone," he growled, his voice dripping with malice. "But you just had to push things too far by involving Shelley."

Eddie's terror was palpable as the demon shadows carried him towards the window. "No - please," he pleaded desperately. He was crying, sobbing actually – his words barely audible.

Nick relished in the fear emanating from his prey, considering ending his life right then and there. "I could kill you- right now, just fling you out the window," he threatened coldly. "And everyone would think it was a suicide."

Just before Nick gave in to his dark desires, Shane and Tommy burst into the room, laughing and joking as usual. The demons released Eddie, and he landed on the floor on his knees; Shane and

Tommy, upon seeing Eddie's terrified state, quickly realized something was amiss and helped him to his feet before ushering him out of the room. Nick stayed on his bed, his twisted satisfaction was evident on his face. He knew that Eddie would tell the others about what happened, and maybe now they would finally leave him alone.

The demon voice in his head whispered sinister suggestions of ways to eliminate all three of his tormentors, unhappy with his decision not to kill Eddie, but Nick restrained himself, prioritizing his larger ambitions and steering clear of any potential legal entanglements- He knew he could get them at any time- he just had to give the order- and this gave him a tremendous feeling of power which satiated him for now.

Determined to succeed, Nick immersed himself in his studies and eventually earned his degree after three years of hard work. However, his accomplishment came with a hefty debt to the government and a growing list of paybacks that he intended to address in due time, guided by the dark whispers of his inner demon.

After graduating, Nick anticipated a smooth transition into the workforce, envisioning multiple job offers from the prestigious law firms he had applied to. He secured a modest apartment in Hunts Point, a promising neighbourhood in the Bronx with affordable rent, even with his part-time job at the markets. However, his plans to relocate to a more desirable location like Manhattan or Brooklyn were put on hold as months and then years passed without any job offers materializing. Despite attending several interviews, he found himself repeatedly passed over, perplexed by the rejection and feeling overlooked. His frustration grew as he questioned why his potential was not recognized and none could or would give him a straight answer. Confident in his intelligence and acting abilities, he believed he possessed all the qualities of a successful lawyer. The dismissive comments from the interviewers only fuelled his resentment, adding more names to his growing list of individuals he felt wronged by. His shifts at the market dwindled to just one night a week, and his rent payments fell behind, intensifying Nick's anger and determination to seek retribution.

And now, today- what a day it had been- He'd had an interview at McAdam, Swaine, and White Law in New York and was rejected on the spot—the bastards told him he lacked personality and seemed somehow amused by this. As he left the building, he saw Shelley walking in. He stopped in his tracks and smiled at her, hoping she

would come over, but she looked at him and then quickly looked away as if she didn't even know him. She swiftly scuttled into the elevator and out of sight.

He thought about Shelley now and smiled a little as he contemplated the rope he was twisting and turning into a perfect noose.

He caught the bus home, standing all the way because it was so crowded, only to get home to an eviction notice plastered on his front door. His thoughts quickly turned to ending it all - "Go on, go on, go

on—do it, do it!" The demon in his head had been encouraging, to say the least.

His rough fingers finished tying the final knot, creating the perfect noose. He stared at it, a simple instrument of escape from the

relentless pain and rejection that had defined his life. The rope felt rough against his hands, an unsettling contrast to the unbearable

smoothness of the nothingness he felt inside. He stood there and let the noose drop in his hand; the noose swayed slightly in the stillness of the room, a silent mocking reminder of his impending decision. The demon's voice in his head grew louder, pushing him closer to the edge. He climbed onto the chair and tied the noose to the railing above his head.

Damn them all to hell! Damn Shelley. Damn Shane, Tommy, and Eddie. Damn those bigwig law firms. Damn the bosses at the Market. Damn the landlord. But most of all, damn his parents for being right!

He mulled over his list of paybacks. Each name etched into his mind like a permanent scar. With trembling hands, he pulled the rough noose over his head and felt its scratchy fibres dig into his skin. A voice in his head whispered, "I'll get them in my next life." He let out a bitter laugh, tasting the bitterness of regret and vengeance on his tongue. And with one final kick, he sent the chair tumbling beneath him as he embraced his fate. The sound of creaking wood echoed in the room, drowned out only by the deafening pounding of his heart in his ears.

The noose tightened around his neck; his body swayed, but the fall was not enough to break his neck. His hands automatically grabbed for the length of rope above him, and his eyes bulged. Unconsciousness came quickly—30 seconds, to be precise. It felt longer. Each second was excruciating - the silence deafening - his body jerked like a waterless fish, and his arms flailed, trying to reach up and grasp the rope. The will to live is strong, even in unconsciousness. Then his arms dropped to his side, and he became still.

His body hung there, a grim testament to his despair. The room seemed to grow colder. The mocking faces of those who had wronged him flashed through his mind one last time, an unholy parade of tormentors. Surely, death would solve all his problems, but it came slowly. Then, finally, his breathing stopped, his heart gave out, and everything faded to black.

In the darkness, a faint light emerged. It was not the peaceful glow of an afterlife but a flickering, ominous flame. Whether it was hellish punishment or something else entirely, he did not know. All he knew was that even in this final act of defiance against the world, he was not free. The pain, the regrets, the anger—they all seemed to follow him into this next existence.

The pressure eased from around Nicholas's neck. He opened his eyes and slowly regained some focus in the darkness. He wasn't hanging now; he was standing in the middle of the room. He wasn't alone either. Standing directly in front of him was a well-dressed stranger with an aura of unnerving confidence; he was extremely tall, at least six foot six, with curly dark hair- tousled and longish. Even in the darkness of the room, Nick could see this tall man clearly. He wore a black suit and a brilliant smile, and his eyes glowed red in the dim room. Had he saved him? Why would he save me? he wondered. No words were spoken out loud, but in his head, Nick heard the tall man answer him in a deep, smooth voice. "I could use a man like you, Nick", he said, "I can help you get everything you ever wanted and more." The smile never left his face.

"I thought I would be dead," said Nick in his head to the tall man.

"You are," said the tall man. "Look behind you." Still, no words were actually spoken. He turned and saw his own limp body hanging behind him. He was still.

Nick's emotions had faded away as he faced the stranger. He couldn't recall a time when he had ever felt so empty. Even the dancing shadows and the one that used to occupy his mind were no longer there.

"Hello, Nicholas," the man said aloud in his smooth, deep voice with a disconcerting smile. "I am Natas".

The man's presence seemed to fill the small apartment with an oppressive energy.

"I couldn't help but sense that you were in need of a …. friend," Natas continued smoothly. "Perhaps someone to guide you, to help with your list..."

Nick frowned, uncertain of what to make of this intrusion. "How do you—why are you here? What do you want?"

"I'm here to help you, Nick. You see, I have a special talent for resolving problems, especially the kind that weighs heavily on the soul."

Nick felt a curious mix of fear and intrigue. Despite the eerie presence, there was something compelling about Natas' words. Confusion and curiosity won over Nick's initial wariness; he felt a strange pull toward this enigmatic visitor.

Natas smiled wider, sensing his influence taking hold.

"Let me show you," he said, his voice dripping with persuasive malevolence.

"If we work together, we can change your world, and I guarantee that you will be rewarded. All I ask is for your trust," Nicholas nodded in agreement, suddenly unable to speak.

Natas' gaze flitted over to the limp body suspended in the background. The chair beneath it had been knocked askew, but with a swift flick of his arms, he repositioned it upright. As if a spell had been broken, the noose around Nicholas's neck gave way, and his lifeless form slumped into the chair.

"Keep a firm grip on me," Natas commanded. The two souls entwined and merged as one, and together they channelled their energy into Nicholas Green's still body, breathing new vitality and vigour back into it. His eyes fluttered open, and he took a deep, shuddering breath as life flooded back into him once more.

***

Nicholas had grown accustomed to the lingering presence of demons, having shared his body and mind with one for as long as he could remember. But this connection, like a bolt of lightning, was unlike anything he had ever felt before. It coursed through him with an intensity that sent shivers down his spine and set his nerves ablaze. He could feel a genuine spark of satanic influence igniting within him. He had opened the door to a force that would not only alter his own destiny but also potentially reshape the fate of the entire world like an imminent storm brewing on the horizon.

THREE

The lab, once a sanctuary of science, now echoed with a sinister silence that settled heavily on Penelope MacDonald's shoulders. She stood there as the last vibrations of Satan's departure trembled through the ground, her heart pounding in rhythm with the aftershocks. Beside her, Finley Menzies and Eligh Browne were statues of dread, their faces etched with the same horror that clawed at her insides. The charred edges of reality frayed before them, revealing the gaping maw where the Devil and his clone had vanished into the bowels of the Earth.

"God, what have we done?" Eligh murmured; the levity drained from his voice like colour from his cheeks.

Penelope's mind raced, desperately seeking a solution to the abyssal problem they could never divulge. To speak of it was to invite death – Satan had been unequivocal in his threats. Her gaze flitted across the ruined lab, the scattered instruments mute witnesses to an unspeakable act. In a moment of harrowing clarity, she knew there was only one way out.

"Tomorrow -we burn it," she whispered, her voice steady despite the quiver of fear that threatened to undo her. "We erase every trace."

Finley's eyes, wide behind his glasses, met hers, understanding blooming in the silent exchange. With their energy spent and bodies weary, they gathered the remnants of their strength and secured their dark secret within the confines of the lab. The resounding click of the door echoed through the empty space as they turned towards the solace of isolation. The group dispersed, each stepping into their own vehicle. They were a blur of shadows and silhouettes in the dim light of the parking lot, their faces etched with exhaustion and the weight of their burden.

Night had wrapped its cloak around the city when Penelope, after a solitary meal and a shower that did nothing to cleanse her conscience, drove back to the now-abandoned science centre. Anticipation bubbled in her chest as she imagined the night ahead.

What if the boys changed their minds? She couldn't bear to wait until tomorrow. In a burst of determination, she vowed to do it tonight - under the cover of darkness. She could already see the flickering flames and feel the heat on her skin as she set the fire herself. And when it was done, she would call the boys and tell them.

She parked blocks away, her steps shadows among shadows, slipping unseen past security's cyclical vigilance. The air hung heavy with the scent of impending ash as she made her way to the heart of the facility, to the lab that bore witness to their damning pact.

Methodical and precise, Penelope set the flames to dance, watching as they consumed the evidence of their sin. The fire crackled with a life of its own, a hungry beast feasting on the carcass of their transgressions. She retreated, the inferno's glow painting an eerie backdrop to her silent escape.

Eligh's house loomed dark and forlorn as she arrived, the place a stark contrast to the flames she left behind. With a trembling hand, she dialled Finley's number, her voice betraying none of the turmoil that roiled beneath the surface.

"Meet me at Eligh's. Now," she said, the urgency clear.

They congregated, three souls adrift in a sea of guilt and fear. Penelope sat, the weight of unspoken deeds pressing upon her chest, as they spoke of futures untethered from the horrors of their past, and she told them what she had done to rectify it.

"Scotland can no longer be our home," she stated, a cold resolve settling over her. "Our paths diverge tonight. It's the only way to survive, the only way to ensure this...abomination remains buried."

Nods of acquiescence bound them in a solemn pact, an unvoiced agreement to sever the ties that could unravel the fragile tapestry of their continued existence. Their words, whispers in the dark, were the final echoes of lives irrevocably altered, a dirge for the souls they had once been.

***

Penelope stood before the glistening expanse of the ocean where she had asked the taxi driver to drop her. The crashing waves provided a soothing respite from the exhausting and never-ending flight to Adelaide that she just endured. The salty breeze tangled through her short, curly brown hair as she looked out at the horizon, where the water kissed the sky in an endless embrace.

Her suitcase stood beside her, filled with more than clothes and personal items—it was laden with the weight of a new beginning. She had always been the one to put work first, her life dictated by the methodical nature of scientific research. But here, now, under the vast Australian sky, Penelope McDonald – now Penny Donald- was allowing herself to indulge in the unfamiliar sensation of putting her well-being before all else.

The decision had been both terrifying and liberating. Back in Scotland, Finley had quietly accepted a teaching position at a university in Birmingham, England, his soft tone barely concealing the undercurrent of excitement about delving into a new environment where his awkwardness might be less pronounced. Eligh, ever the talkative optimist, accepted a teaching position in Marseille and had laughed heartily as he recounted the bureaucratic hurdles he faced while securing his French citizenship—a process that seemed designed to test even his usually boundless patience.

"Life," Eligh had joked in his energetic manner, "is the most persistent of teachers, and I am but its humble student."

And so, they had dispersed, each seeking refuge from the darkness that had clawed at the edges of their former lives. Now, as Penelope inhaled deeply, tasting freedom and brine on her tongue, she could feel the last tendrils of that darkness attempting to cling to her soul. She would not allow it to take root again.

Here, she would immerse herself in the study of Yoga, embracing the serenity it offered. For years, she had found solace in the practice, its principles of mindfulness and balance, a counterpoint to the rigorous demands of her analytical mind.

"Survival is not merely about continuing to exist," she reminded herself, echoing the thoughts that had guided her here. Her voice, calm and measured, carried conviction borne from the ashes of her past. "It's about thriving, about choosing a path that fosters growth amid despair."

As if to affirm her resolve, the sun dipped lower, casting a golden glow over the waters. Penelope took it as a sign, a beacon guiding her towards a future where she could heal and, perhaps, find peace.

She turned from the ocean, her eyes scanning the quaint seaside suburb of Somerton Park that she would now call home. She picked up her suitcase and stepped forward, her journey beginning with a single determined stride. Her house was just a few short meters from the stunning beach that promised peaceful days and tranquil nights.

The salty sea air filled her nostrils, bringing with it a sense of calm and freedom.

This was her time, her chance to redefine what it meant to fully live. Yes, this was the perfect place for her to start anew. She would grasp it with both hands, holding on even as the shadows of yesterday sought to drag her back into the abyss.

FOUR

As the sun began to rise, Nicholas woke up in a daze, unsure if the events of the previous night had been nothing but a strange dream. He reached up to touch the skin around his neck and immediately winced at the pain. It felt swollen, raw, and sore to the touch. Before he could think too much about it, he heard a voice speaking from within him - a smooth, low voice that seemed oddly familiar. With a jolt, he was fully awake. Natas urged him to hurry, but Nicholas fought for control of his body. He stumbled out of bed and into the bathroom to shower and brush the furry feeling from his teeth. He touched the stubble on his face and neck, and it reminded him of the chafing sensation, causing him to dismiss the idea of shaving. Plus, in a strange way, the scruff would hide some of the chafing and redness. As he caught a glimpse of himself in the mirror through the foggy steam, he noticed a faint red glow emanating from his body. Before he could investigate further, Natas took over and led him out of the tiny bathroom.

He peered through the open bedroom door, and his eyes fell upon an unknown man standing inside the kitchen. The sight caused him to momentarily forget about the strange glowing light he had seen moments before as he focused on this new and unexpected presence. The man stood with an air of authority, dressed in khakis reminiscent of a military uniform but not quite fitting the mould. His tall, muscular frame was accentuated by close-cropped hair that was shaved in strict military fashion. His arms were crossed over his chest, and he leaned against the front door with a stoic expression on his face, unmoving and vigilant.

A dark cloud surrounded the man, making Nick feel uneasy. "Morning, boss," he said, his voice low and smooth. He gestured towards the bed, where a perfectly pressed Gucci suit, a crisp black shirt, and shiny Prada loafers were laid out neatly. Natas spoke aloud for the first time. His voice being deeper than Nick's own, sent shivers down his spine. "Is everything ready?" he asked, to which the stranger nodded.

"Yes, sir. Natas, sir"

It was then that Nick realized he was no longer in control of his own body. He was merely a spectator as Natas took over like a skilled driver behind the wheel of a car.

After quickly dressing, he exited the apartment, not bothering to shut the door behind him. A sleek black SUV was parked outside, and the stranger who had been in his apartment opened the door for him. Natas climbed into the car with confidence, and they drove towards New York City at high speed.

Calvin chatted nonstop as they navigated through the early morning traffic, giving Nick bits and pieces of information about their destination and the purpose of their journey. According to Calvin, they had been preparing for this moment for quite some time - awaiting the arrival of a person with special abilities granted by Satan himself.

Nick listened intently, but what caught his attention more than anything else were the people they passed on the streets - each one surrounded by colourful clouds that seemed to pulse with energy. At first, he thought it was just his imagination, but as they got closer to the city and there were more and more people, he knew it was real. It was unlike anything he had ever seen before.

Natas settled back into the plush, smooth leather seat and took his time explaining the auras that Nick could now see. With a gentle sweep of his hand, he pointed out the young ones - the babies and children that shone with the brightest golden light. These pure souls had not yet chosen their paths in life - good or evil. "Those are the ones we want, Nick," Natas stated with a sly smile. "They will always come easily, for they have no concept of evil. And as children, they are expected to live long lives, so they have no angels around them to protect them. They are easy prey for us."

His voice grew sinister as he continued, "At precisely the right moment when we take one of their souls, a demon will enter their small bodies. Gradually, as we gather enough of these innocent souls, the whole world will turn evil as they grow and mature into adults. The ageing population will be too weak to fight us - if they haven't already passed on." He paused for emphasis before adding, "For this is why we are here - to fast-track the taking of these young souls." The golden soul will then be taken to hell and will eventually become part of Satan's army.

Natas went on to explain the auras of everyday people - how each one revealed what kind of person they were. The rainbow of colours glowed brightly, while others were grey or black.

As Nick gazed at the crowd, Natas went on to explain in detail- the grey auras that surrounded some individuals, were the embodiment of evil- murderers, rapists, and paedophiles lurking among the unsuspecting crowd. In contrast, there were those with black auras who were already possessed by demons.

But amidst the darkness, there was a spectrum of pastel colours shining brightly. Shades of orange, blue, pink, green, and purple represented the everyday people- not particularly good or evil, just living their lives. Natas referred to them as "the common people," a term that made Nick smile inwardly.

His voice dripped with malice as he outlined the plan - a sinister plot to taint every soul and gain ultimate power over the world. They had carefully orchestrated this scheme, weaving their dark intentions into the fabric of society. The very thought sent a shiver down his spine.

"The souls that are taken to the underworld 'mature' at different rates, and the golden ones are by far the slowest; their glow will gradually fade as the years go by, but it will take twenty whole years before they turn. There is no transformation to any other colour, but they will eventually turn black and be just as loyal to Satan as the demons who chose to serve him- The pastels are merely food for the demons- if we can get them."

Nick's eyes stung at the sight of two rare beings who radiated with pure white light, their brightness almost blinding. Natas grunted- these are the white lighters- protected by angels," he went on to explain; these were the true heroes of the world- healers and life-savers like doctors, nurses, police officers, and firefighters. They could also be religious figures like priests or other do-gooders. But Natas warned him not to be fooled by appearances; even among the so-called 'religious' individuals, there could still be hidden darkness. The bright lights were earned through actions and deeds, not just beliefs.

These special individuals had angels protecting them at all times, Natas explained. They were untouchable even by the mightiest of demons; one Angel alone was more powerful and imposing than a hundred demons combined.

Natas then proceeded to share an ancient story with Nick - a legend passed down through the ages. It was said that when Satan was first banished to rule the underworld, he sent some of his most cunning and ruthless demons to the earth with a mission to bring him more souls. Among these demons was one known as 'Azeazel', who foolishly underestimated the true power of the Angels.

In his arrogance, Azeazel thought it would be easier to steal an Angel's soul as it left its human vessel rather than seeking out an Angel-less dying person. He chose a sickly woman in her eighties whose light shone brightly - she had been a skilled nurse in her mortal life and was now on her deathbed. Azeazel believed it would be a simple task to overpower such a small angel when the time came.

But as he approached the departing soul, Azeazel came face to face with the Angel himself. In a rare moment of fierce emotion, the usually serene and composed Angel transformed into a towering figure twice his size. His face contorted into that of a fanged serpent, and he let out a blood-curdling scream that echoed throughout the heavens and beyond.

Hearing this cry for help, other angels rushed to aid their kin. But by the time they arrived, Azeazel had already been crushed by the sheer force of the Angel's enormous wings. The battle between good and evil was swift, brutal, and absolute. Evil was defeated.

Azeazel, once a powerful demon, was now nothing but ash and smoke. His remains swirled in the air, a chaotic dance of black and red, his essence, then scattered across the infernal realms with a single flap of the angel's wings. The angels' warning echoed through the dark abyss, a reminder to all demons who dared challenge their divine authority.

Since that fateful encounter, demons have learned to tread cautiously around those touched by divine light. And the white glow that surrounds these special individuals is not just a mere aura - it is the radiant light of an angel's wings wrapped protectively around them. "Avoid them," Natas warned Nick. He shivered at the thought of crossing paths with such powerful beings.

Satan chose you himself, Natas told Nick- and of course, Nick wanted to know why, "Satan was impressed by you over and over, and he kept watch always. He knew you would leave the ordinary world early; he watched patiently, waiting for an opportunity, and when it arose, he did not hesitate to send me in, so now, here I am, and we can work together to bring the world into darkness so Satan can walk amongst us as the great lord and mighty ruler this world has been in search of."

Nick fell silent as he took in all this information. He watched the aura clouded people through the car window, surprised at the many dark figures moving amongst them all and the few bright ones. Clearly, Satan's work had already started.

The steady drone of Calvin's chatter in the front seat broke through Nick's thoughts. Calvin seemed overly cheerful for someone enveloped in this dark mission, but his energy was infectious, making Nick feel more awake and alert.

As they neared the towering skyline of New York City, Natas grew increasingly quiet as if gathering himself for the tasks ahead. Nick could feel a change within him as well, a heightened awareness, a tingling sense of otherworldliness.

The sleek black SUV glided to a stop at the grand entrance of The Glitz Hotel, its glossy exterior shimmering in the warm morning sunlight. The chrome accents caught the light and sparkled like diamonds, giving off an air of luxury and opulence. Bellhops in impeccable uniforms rushed forward with a friendly smile, eager to assist their prestigious guests. He emerged from the vehicle with a confident stride, his commanding presence causing heads to turn and eyes to linger. Behind his charming façade, a hint of dark purpose lurked, unnoticed by those around him.

Natas surged with satisfaction at the sight of the extravagant hotel. The auras around him grew brighter and more defined as they approached the doors, each one pulsating with its own unique energy like a symphony of colours. Nick couldn't help but steal glances at some of the hotel staff, noting the range of auras surrounding them. Most were soft pastel hues, indicating their roles as ordinary people going about their daily lives. But there were a lot that carried grey or blackened auras, hinting at darker secrets hidden beneath their surface. Amidst them all, Nick saw glowing white auras here and there - rare sightings of pure goodness amidst a sea of mundane and darkness.

Calvin swiftly guided them to the elevator, heading up to the thirty-third (top) floor where their lavish suite awaited. The ride up was mingled with tension and anticipation.

The elevator doors opened to reveal a lavish space of opulence and luxury. Brilliant crystal chandeliers hung from the ceiling, casting a warm glow across the room. The walls were adorned with exquisite pieces of fine art, each one more stunning than the last. Natas led them forward, his steps purposeful as he guided Nick towards the grand windows that overlooked the bustling city below. An air of satisfaction radiated from the demon spirit within him as if basking in a small victory in this extravagant setting.

"We have much to do," Natas spoke in a voice that was both Nick's own thoughts and something otherworldly. "We will rest briefly, but then we must strategize."

Nick nodded, feeling both exhilarated and terrified by this new reality. The weight of it all pressed heavily on his shoulders as they settled into the luxurious surroundings. Calvin wasted no time in ordering a lavish spread of room service delicacies. His stomach growling with anticipation- Nick sank into a plush lounge chair while they waited. As soon as the sumptuous feast arrived, he feasted like a king, relishing the abundance of savoury and sweet dishes that tantalized his taste buds. The aroma of freshly prepared food filled the air, adding to the luxurious atmosphere of their hotel room. Each bite was a burst of flavour, from the delicate spices to the rich sauces that coated his palate.

But Natas was eager for action once again, and before long, he announced, "Soon, we will act, and the next steps of our plan will unfold." With those words lingering in the air, Nick closed his eyes momentarily and contemplated how his world had irrevocably changed. As the morning light filtered into the suite, he braced himself for whatever lay ahead.

Natas stood tall and commanding as demons disguised as businessmen in sleek suits filed in one by one, bowing their heads in deference to their leader. They spent the morning and half of the afternoon as they discussed plans for the church that had been meticulously prepared for Natas' arrival. Each detail was carefully considered and debated, with Natas giving precise orders and making sure every aspect was perfectly aligned with his grand vision.

"We won't be needing the car," he told Calvin as they left the apartment late that afternoon. The bustling streets of New York City greeted them, and word spread quickly - with people from all walks of life drawn to him, the enigmatic figure known as the Black Lord.

They had come from far and wide in anticipation of his arrival, their eyes filled with reverence and awe.

Nick strode confidently through the throngs of followers. His trademark crimson aura radiated powerfully from his being, drawing people in and leaving them yearning for a connection to their leader. As he passed by, people reached out to touch him, their fingers grazing his skin in a desperate attempt to feel a piece of his power. Calvin, walking a few steps behind, seemed unfazed by the adoration lavished upon his boss.

Natas grinned as he walked, relishing in the attention and explaining to Nick the reason behind his followers' desire to "touch" him.

"With a single touch, I can fulfil any material desire my followers have. Whether it's a better job, a luxurious house, a luxury car, or designer clothes - all they need to do is make contact with my aura and focus on their craving." The air crackled with an unearthly energy radiating from Natas, drawing in his devotees with hypnotic allure. They reached out for his hands and face, believing his skin to be the source of his miraculous gifts, their fingers trembling with a mix of fear and reverence.

As they passed a mirrored window, Nick caught sight of his own reflection and was taken aback. His aura glowed a deep crimson, pulsing with energy. He noticed that he seemed taller somehow, as if the darkness inside him had stretched him out. His eyes shone red, a clear indication of his true nature.

Despite his desire to stop and examine himself further, Natas continued on without hesitation. As they approached their destination, an old, dilapidated church on Seventh Avenue, Nick's eyes were drawn to the large crowd gathered outside. Eager faces turned towards the entrance, awaiting their leader's arrival. And behind them, a throng of devoted followers trailed along.

As the sun fell lower in the sky, the abandoned church stood before them, its crumbling exterior a testament to years of neglect. The paint was peeling and cracked, giving way to patches of old bricks and weathered wood. Weeds and vines crept up the sides of the building, reclaiming it as their own.

Natas and Calvin slipped in through a discreet side door. Their presence causing the bustling crowd to halt and fall silent without any prompt.

Natas and Calvin walked towards the double doors at the front of the church, their footsteps echoed through the church. The crowd, a sea of eager faces, erupted into cheers as the doors were flung open, revealing the grand interior of the church.

As they made their way down the aisle, the hush of anticipation fell over the crowd. They were ready to follow their Black Lord's every command.

The inside of the church was a sight to behold. Sunlight streamed through red stained-glass windows, casting an otherworldly glow upon the scene. While some of the windows were partially boarded up from the outside, delicate beams of light still managed to pierce through them, adding to the ethereal atmosphere. The floors gleamed with a polished finish, and the rows upon rows of pews were recently stained a rich mahogany colour. At the front of the church, a pristine white marble altar stood proudly, reflecting hints of red from the glowing windows.

With a commanding presence, Natas addressed his devoted followers. The church was so packed that people spilled out into the aisles and even into the carpark outside. But despite the tight quarters, all eyes remained fixated on their Black Lord and his words.

The air was thick with anticipation as Natas' deep, velvety voice cut through the silence. "In darkness, we rise - welcome!" he declared, his words carrying weight and power.

"We welcome the darkness" the crowd chanted back in unison. Their voices echoed through the room as they eagerly waited for their leader's instructions.

"I am Nicholas Green... Nick to all of my friends," he continued, a charming smile spreading across his face. "And I 'DO' hope we are all friends."

His piercing gaze swept over the sea of black and grey auras emanating from every member of his congregation. But just beyond the doors, he could see a few golden auras shining brightly - children brought by their parents to be the first sacrifices to Natas. They were strategically placed far enough back that they wouldn't hear everything but close enough to feel the dark energy emanating from the congregation.

His sermon was long and captivating, filled with promises of a glorious future under his rule. The room was silent, save for occasional cheers and applause at appropriate moments. No one dared to interrupt or question their leader's plans - the fear of his wrath was palpable.

He spoke of his plans to build churches all over the world and carefully handpick leaders who would prove themselves worthy of such an esteemed role. The audience shuddered at the thought of being chosen and wondered if they could ever live up to Natas' expectations. As they hung on every word, it was clear that their devotion to him was unwavering.

At last, the time had come for Natas to demonstrate how his work would be carried out. He called for a golden soul and the room parted like the Red Sea, as a young girl, no more than four years old, was led through the crowd by her father to the altar. Natas was charming and charismatic as ever, greeting her with a warm smile and speaking softly in his rich, deep voice. Immediately, he put the little girl at ease, and she willingly walked into his outstretched arms.

With great care, Natas lifted the child onto the altar and laid her down gently. Her dark brown eyes never left his face, filled with trust and innocence. But as he held her pinned firmly to the altar - one hand on her stomach and the other across her mouth and nose - her eyes bulged slightly in fear. He spoke softly to her the whole time he held her there, and she barely struggled against him. Her death came relatively quick.

Nick watched as the golden aura of the girl's soul floated away from her body, quickly seized by what he now knew to be soul seekers - demons that appeared as nothing but shadows, always lurking nearby, waiting for their next victim. The soul seekers dragged the bright light of the girl's soul down and through the floorboards, presumably to hell. As this took place, another soul seeker entered her lifeless body, slipping in at the precise moment her bright soul departed. Natas removed his hand from her face, and the little girl gasped for air, sitting upright once again.

To the onlookers, she appeared unharmed - her heart beating and breath steady - but Nick could see the emptiness behind her dull, lifeless eyes, her once golden aura now a dull black. The crowd broke out in applause as she walked back into the waiting arms of her father.

Another brilliant, golden aura surrounded a teenager as he was brought to Natas. The light shone down on his small frame, illuminating him like a beacon amidst the bustling crowd.

In a bulky wheelchair, he made his way through the crowds as they shifted to let him pass. His legs, hidden beneath a crocheted blanket, were thin and delicate, a stark contrast to the bustling energy of the crowd around him. It was clear that he was not able to walk on his own, but his spirit seemed unbreakable as he took in the sights and sounds of the bustling event.

Walking beside him were his parents, their grey auras blending in with the swarms of people around them. As they approached Natas, the father kept his head bowed while softly asking if the ritual could restore his son's ability to walk. Natas' eyes gleamed with delight, catching the attention of the parents as they lifted their faces towards him.

Bending down with care, Natas scooped the boy into his arms and addressed the crowd. "Watch, my fellow dark walkers," he proclaimed, "I will give this boy back his legs! There is no ailment I cannot cure. Let this display convince you to bring in common people as well - we strive to help ALL children, whether they are sick, injured, depressed, or misbehaving. I can aid them all!"

With slow and deliberate movements, Natas circled around the altar before placing the boy down gently. The boy maintained eye contact with Natas as he tenderly brushed away stray strands of hair from his face. Then, with one hand over his mouth and nose and the other firmly holding him down on the altar, Natas began the ritual. Talking softly to the boy as his eyes widened in silent protest, but he did not resist.

Time seemed to stand still for the boy and the quiet observers as Natas held him in this position. In reality, it was only a few minutes before Natas could see the golden light of the boy's aura rising from his injured form and the presence of a soul seeker entering.

With a swift motion, he lifted his hand and stroked the boy's hair once more. Invisibly, two soul seekers dragged the vibrant golden soul down through the floorboards - a sight that only Natas (and Nick) could see.

The young boy took a deep breath and sat up with the gentle assistance of Natas. His chest heaved, his small frame trembling with exhaustion and pain. Speaking softly, Natas said,

"Your legs may be weak now, but they will grow strong again,"

With Natas' support, the boy slowly stood up, his legs wobbling beneath him. He took a few hesitant steps towards his waiting parents, who were both overcome with emotion- tears streaming down their faces. They each took one of his hands and guided him through the parted crowd, who stood in awe and admiration at the boy's transformation.

The crowd erupted into thunderous applause and cheers as they made their way out of the church into the night.

Natas' piercing gaze swept over the devoted crowd, his words dripping with conviction and fervour. "Invite all your friends and acquaintances. Spread the word about YOUR church- the Church of Ancient Souls and tell everyone who will listen about my unparalleled healing powers." He paused for effect before adding, "In darkness, we rise!"

The crowd erupted in a chorus of "We welcome the darkness!"

After the crowd quieted once more, Natas beckoned three additional children onto the stage with a simple gesture of his hand, summoning them one by one. Each one radiated a dazzling golden aura, their innocent faces filled with trust and belief in their leader. As he began his ritual once again, Nick could feel the dark energy pulsating through his body with practiced ease, Natas smothered them until their golden auras dissipated, replaced by the ominous darkness of a soul seeker.

The timing of this switch had to be precise, and Nick watched from the back seat of his mind as each transformation was executed flawlessly.

A bolt of lightning shot up his spine, sending a chill through his body as he witnessed the true manifestation of immense strength and power.

The sacrifices were carried out with terrifying precision, fuelling the frenzied cheers and applause of the enraptured crowd. It was not just a display of their beloved leader's incredible powers but an affirmation of their unwavering devotion and blind worship.

As the final notes of the sermon faded into the air, Natas made his way back to the open doors of the church. He stood tall and proud in the doorway, his aura radiating with an unseen energy. As his devoted congregation filed out, many of the grey-aura people reached out to touch his hands or face. He smiled knowingly, hiding the true nature of his work- The moment they made contact with him, their auras darkened slightly, inching them closer to eternal servitude under the dark lord.

FIVE

s the months went by, the 'Church of Ancient Souls' was flourishing. Nick scanned his congregation and noticed a diverse array of auras. Only those with the bright white auras were excluded; Natas welcomed everyone else and, true to his word, healed their children from a wide range of ailments, from blindness to mischief and everything in between. However, Nick grew increasingly restless, fixating on his 'list' of individuals he sought to avenge and wondering if Natas had forgotten his promise to assist him. Though aware of Nick's thoughts, Natas remained focused on expanding the church.

With meticulous precision, he hand-picked each new Minister and personally trained them in his methods of "healing," preparing them to establish new branches across the country. And beyond that, he had even grander plans - to spread his teachings overseas. England, Spain, France, and other parts of Europe, as well as China, India, and Australia, were all on his ambitious agenda. But for the time being, he focused on finding suitable "Churches" to expand his influence across the United States.

Natas regularly held conferences with demons disguised as businessmen, their dark suits and polished shoes exuding an air of importance. They came from all corners of the world, their foreign accents filling the conference room at the Glitz Hotel with a cacophony of voices. As they discussed business matters, Nick's mind often wandered to his mental list of payback targets, each one burning with a desire for revenge.

The warmth of summer seeped through the open door to the balcony. Nick restlessly paced around his luxurious suite, his payback list on his mind. Finally, Natas brought up the topic that he had been eagerly anticipating, causing his heart to quicken with excitement.

"I have information on Shelley Knights," Natas said, and Nick's heart raced with hope.

Admitting his love for Shelley had been a long time coming, and he often tried to push her from his mind. But deep down, he knew it was futile. He couldn't deny the intense longing he felt for her any longer. In his past life, she had haunted his dreams and fuelled countless fantasies. No matter how hard he tried to push her out of his mind, she always found a way to seep back in, like an alluring siren luring him towards inevitable heartache. Now, at the mention of her name, his heart lurched with a glimmer of hope.

Nick was firm as he addressed Natas, "I don't want any harm to come to her- and I certainly don't want her soul tainted," he stated. "I want her to be mine- my wife."

"Yes, it shall be done. We can be quite charming when necessary," he replied. "And rest assured, I will ensure that her soul remains untainted." The air around them seemed to crackle with otherworldly energy as they made plans for the young woman's future.

***

Shelley Knights hurried towards the multi-story glass office building that housed McAdam, Swaine, and White Lawyers. She emerged from the bustling city streets, her body draped in a tight dark grey dress suit that hugged her hourglass figure. Matching heels clicked against the pavement as she hurriedly made her way towards her destination. Her blonde locks were swept up into a low chignon, exposing the graceful curve of her neck. She was in such a hurry that she nearly passed Nick without even noticing. He was leaning against a pillar outside, looking relaxed and nonchalant.

A sincere smile lit up Nick's face as Shelley's eyes suddenly locked into his, and her steps faltered. "Nick," she exclaimed breathlessly, feeling a slight flush rise to her cheeks.

Nick maintained his cool demeanour, though inside, he could hardly contain his excitement at seeing her again after all this time. "Oh, hi Shelley," he replied casually, his heart racing. They struck up a casual conversation, making it seem like a chance encounter, but he had planned the whole thing down to the last detail. After a few minutes, with a confident smile that made his dimples deepen, he asked her if she would like to join him for dinner later. How could anyone resist his charms? Especially now that he had Natas ready to back him up if needed - not that he planned on needing it. He was determined to win her over on his own.

Their date was a resounding success. They dined at the exclusive

46

restaurant, Le Sarnardin, located on Fifty-First Street. Thanks to Natas' connections, they easily secured a reservation, impressing Shelley with their effortless access. After dinner, they took a leisurely walk through the nearby central park, arm in arm, as Nick displayed chivalrous manners.

She was completely engrossed by his every word as he shared details about his new role as the Pastor of the Church of Ancient Souls. He spoke passionately about his work, giving no indication of its true, sinister purpose- even going so far as to tell her how he had decided against becoming a lawyer because of their corrupt practices.

The evening came to a close. He kissed her gently at her doorstep and said goodnight. Without looking back, he walked away, leaving Shelley longing for more of his company.

Nick strolled back toward the Glitz Hotel, feeling satisfied with the evening. He could feel Natas discord within, he felt restless and angry- Nick realised quickly Natas was horny- he could not control the blood pulsing through him and the rage that was rising within as well- he wanted to have Shelley that night, and Nick just let her go... for the first time they wrestled internally. By the time they reached the elevator, Natas was furious, and once the doors closed, his aura rose from Nick's body darker than ever and towered over him in his full Demonic shape. Nick did not back down, and they argued until they reached the top floor- "No- we are not harming Shelley!" Nick yelled.

Natas' words were sharp, his tone dripping with superiority. "You don't understand what it means to rule," he spat. "You take what you want without question, without hesitation." He spoke with a ruthless determination, making it clear that there was no room for negotiation in his version of leadership- But Nick refused to give in.

"She will be my WIFE!" he declared, his anger growing stronger than ever. Not often did they both speak out loud. The two voices coming from one body would have seemed bizarre to anyone listening. Their voices echoed off the metal walls, each word a sharp weapon in their heated argument. The confined space of the elevator seemed to intensify their emotions, making their words ring out like a battle cry. They were trapped in this small box, unable to escape from the tension and anger that filled the air. The ding of each passing floor felt like a countdown to an inevitable explosion. The elevator came to a halt, and as soon as the doors dinged open, they both fell silent.

After leaving the elevator and stepping into the room, Natas took a moment to compose himself, and his usual faint red aura reappeared as his anger subsided; it was then he noticed a young woman clad in the hotel's maid uniform standing with Calvin near the window. Despite the late hour, she was diligently checking to see if there were any additional needs for the lord. Her dark aura seemed to radiate from her as Natas abruptly interrupted their conversation, his smile devious and filled with intent. The young woman returned his smile, flattered by the hunger she could see in his eyes.

With a sharp wave of his hand, Natas instructed Calvin to leave the room. As Calvin made his way to the open elevator, Natas roughly grabbed the pretty young woman by the back of her hair, causing her to gasp in surprise. She felt like a doll in his grip, powerless against his strong hold. The feeling of flattery quickly turned to fear as he covered her mouth with his and kissed her roughly, his other hand lifting her skirt and ripping away her delicate underwear.

There was no tenderness or care in his actions as he turned her around and forcefully took her from behind over the arm of a nearby couch. It was a quick and brutal encounter, filled with pain and terror for the young woman. And just as suddenly as it began, it was over. Natas put both hands on each side of her head, and with a sharp twist, he snapped her neck, killing her instantly. He dropped her lifeless body to the floor without another word.

Not bothering to look back at the lifeless woman, Natas casually zipped up his pants and left the room with a calm demeanour. He strolled into the expansive bedroom, unfazed by what had just happened.

As if on cue, Calvin returned to the room and quickly made

arrangements to have the young maid's body removed. Natas lay on the bed, sated and pleased with himself.

As Nick drifted off to sleep, his mind replayed the events of the evening- first his date with Shelley, which had exceeded all his expectations. But it soon fixated on the twisted satisfaction he felt from taking the life of the attractive young maid. He revelled in the power and control he had over another human being, relishing in the adrenaline rush that came with taking a life. It was a feeling that he could never fully explain or understand, but it was addictive. The twisted feeling was one that he couldn't deny had felt undeniably good in the moment. As he drifted into a peaceful sleep, he rejoiced in the comforting embrace of dark euphoria.

As the months went by, Nick continued to woo Shelley with lavish outings - fancy restaurants, movies, and long walks through the city. They would often spend nights curled up on the couch together-basking in the warmth of their growing relationship. Despite his strong attraction to Shelley, Nick respected her wishes to take things slow and never pressured her for more intimacy. He was always a perfect gentleman around her, lulling her into a sense of security-making her feel safe and cherished.

But as their relationship blossomed, a dark and sinister pattern began to emerge. Each time Nick left Shelley's side, Natas would emerge and commit heinous acts of violence against unsuspecting victims. At first, it was women alone who fell prey to Natas' insatiable desires. He would strike in parks, hotels, alleyways - anywhere he could find an easy target. But one night, he raped a young man in the park, and Nick realized that Natas had no sexual preference; he was driven solely by his twisted desire for power and control over others.

After each brutal act, Natas would discard his victims without a second thought and continue on with his day as if nothing had happened.

With an ever-watchful eye, Calvin lurked nearby, ready to dispose of the lifeless bodies with a chillingly calculated efficiency. Like a silent reaper, he would make the grisly task seem effortless, leaving behind no trace or evidence of his actions. Nick couldn't ignore the fact that these violent acts coincided with every moment he spent with Shelley. Natas was growing impatient with the slow progress of their relationship, and Nick wondered if the rapes and killings would ever stop - or had they just become the new normal.

Lying in his bed a few months into his relationship with Shelley, Nick thought about how content he felt now that she was back in his life. He had never truly known happiness before, and it was like experiencing a whole new sensation. She had captured his heart during their university years, but she was unattainable back then in his past life.

Now, however, with Natas' assistance, things had changed, and he knew it was just a matter of time before they would be married.

His mind wandered, remembering how Shelley had entranced

him- Her compassion, wit, and beauty were unmatched, and Nick couldn't envision a future without her now. Natas had granted him complete authority in this aspect of his life - a privilege that Nick relished. He convinced himself that he could manage Natas and vowed to never let him harm Shelley.

Yet, if he were truly honest with himself, he couldn't deny the twisted satisfaction he felt after each 'date' with Shelley. Lying in bed, his mind would often replay the events of the night - like yesterday's- the delightful dinner date with Shelley and then the stark contrast of the brutal rape and murder that Natas carried out afterward. He had to admit he enjoyed the intoxicating thrill of it all. As he drifted off to sleep, the thrill of the rape came back to him- the young man's face was handsome and youthful, with a strong jawline and sharp cheekbones. At first, his eyes were filled with joy and recognition as he saw his Lord, but they were quickly stretched wide in terror. His blonde hair was wild and tousled from the struggle against Natas. He could see the fear in his eyes as Natas dragged him down a dark alleyway, tearing off his clothes while he begged for his life, the desperate heaving of his chest as he gasped for air while Natas took him from behind. The way his arms flailed and thrashed in a futile attempt to fight for survival - these were the images that danced through Nick's mind. And then came the final cracking of the young man's neck as Natas finished with him. As always, Natas left the body without a second glance. As they made their way out of the alleyway, they passed Calvin, tasked with disposing of the body. The young man's soul had long since been claimed by hell with the help of the ever-present soul seekers.

He lay there; a giddy grin grew on his lips, and his heart swelled with excitement. He held onto hope that Natas would continue to manipulate these events, snatching up souls for his own twisted pleasure. There was a dark part of him that relished this cruel game, seeing it as the ultimate form of gratification. He couldn't deny the rush that came with his newfound sense of power and dominance while under Natas' influence. He wondered if this feeling would ever fade or if it would consume him entirely. Still smiling, he drifted off to sleep.

After six long months of dating and 'taking things slowly' as Shelley liked to call it, she finally gave herself to him on a warm, starlit evening. As they slowly undressed each other, Nick's hands were gentle but firm as they explored every inch of her body, savouring the softness of her skin. He entered her, and she let out a moan of pure ecstasy and wrapped her arms tightly around him. Each thrust sent waves of pleasure coursing through her body, her senses overwhelmed with the intensity of their lovemaking. He rode her with an uninhibited passion, his hands exploring every inch of her skin as they moved together in perfect rhythm. The heat between them was palpable, filling the air with an intoxicating energy. And in that moment, they were lost in each other, two bodies becoming one in a whirlwind of desire.

Unbeknownst to Shelley- A fierce battle raged within Nick as he fought to keep Natas at bay. His muscles tensed and strained against Natas' relentless pull, but through sheer willpower, he won out as he brought Shelley to the peak of bliss, and finally, with a deep groan, he released his own pleasure inside her. As they lay together in the warm afterglow, Nick could sense a quiet satisfaction emanating from Natas, pleased with their shared experience. After that, whenever Shelley was near, Natas seemed to withdraw and allow Nick to take control.

Their relationship blossomed naturally as Nick's genuine affection won over Shelley's heart.

Things were going better than he could have imagined with Shelley, so Natas turned his attention to the remaining names on Nick's revenge list, determined to settle all debts.

The unsuspecting city of New York was bustling with the chaos and commotion of a busy Monday morning. Amidst the flurry of people, Natas unleashed his demons to wreak havoc on the unsuspecting law firms that had rejected Nick's dreams of becoming a lawyer. The fires roared and raged like beasts, hungrily consuming everything in their path. The smoke billowed into the sky, ominously darkening the once-bright morning.

As news reporters arrived at the scene, they were struck with awe as they declared it a scene unlike anything ever witnessed in the history of New York. The destruction was staggering, leaving the city reeling in shock and disbelief.

Despite initial speculations, it appeared that the fires were not deliberately lit. And yet, all five law firms were reduced to ashes simultaneously - a coincidence too strange to ignore. The largest number of casualties occurred at McAdam, Swaine, and White law firm - Shelley's place of employment. Little did she know that her absence from the office on this fateful day had been carefully orchestrated by Nick for his vengeful plans.

From his luxurious suite at the Glitz Hotel, Nick sat with a twisted smile as he watched the horizon, ablaze with smoke and flames from the buildings he had set alight. Each flicker of orange and red brought him a sense of satisfaction as his revenge list grew shorter with each burning structure. The sounds of chaos and destruction could be heard from the balcony, fuelling his malicious glee. He took a sip of expensive scotch and chuckled to himself, revelling in the chaos he had caused. At this moment, he felt untouchable and powerful, revelling in the chaos he had created.

The progress of his list was a source of immense satisfaction for Nick. Months ago, he had doubted if Natas would ever fulfill his promises, but now he knew that their plans were finally coming to fruition. All he had to do was be patient.

The destruction of McAdam, Swaine and White Law firm brought a malicious satisfaction to Nick. Flames engulfed the building with an insatiable hunger, devouring everything in its path. Fourteen lawyers, including the firm's namesakes - McAdam, Swaine, and White - perished in the inferno, along with other high-profile staff members. The cold flames of vengeance showed no mercy as they swept through the office.

As Shelley grappled with the shock and horror of losing her colleagues and the familiarity of her routine now reduced to ashes, Nick was there to console her. He held her tightly, whispering words of comfort as she wept. In the wake of the tragedy, their bond grew tighter. Nick's strong, steady presence became her anchor amidst the tempestuous sea of grief that threatened to swallow her whole- even as he secretly revelled in the sweet taste of revenge against those who had wronged him.

Just days after the New York fires that had claimed five highprofile law firms, Nick was once again riveted to his television screen, eagerly watching the news unfold- The reporter's voice cracked with emotion as they described the series of fires that had ravaged the market where Nick had once worked, taking the lives of three people including his former boss and his bitch wife. His heart soared as they showed footage of the apartment building in Hunts Point, where he had rented a derelict apartment not so long ago. The flames had engulfed the entire building, claiming the lives of eleven more people, including the super and landlord who lived in luxury on the top floor. Despite the devastation, the reporter insisted that there was no evidence of foul play or connection between the two fires. However, Nick was not fooled; he knew the connection, and he was jubilant to see more and more names being crossed off his list.

Satan's frustration grew as the months dragged on, each passing moment a reminder of his clone's slow progress on earth. His mission to implant the golden-souled children with demons had started off promising, with golden auras appearing in hell intermittently, but now it seemed his clone was distracted by Nicholas Green's infamous "list." The dark lord scowled, his anger boiling beneath his skin like molten lava as he waited for updates from his underling. How long would it take for him to complete such a simple task? The fiery pits of hell beckoned, and Satan seethed with impatience. He tapped his fingers against the smooth surface of the obsidian table, his dark eyes fixed on the vision pool in front of him. The water rippled and glowed with an intense, otherworldly energy, reflecting the sinister figure leaning over it. He watched as Nicholas Green- Natas' vessel, held his love's hand tightly as they gazed upon the aftermath of the fire that Natas had instigated at the law firm of McAdam, Swaine, and White. Images of chaos and destruction danced before them- buildings reduced to ash, people sobbing. But Natas had a more important mission- to claim the golden souls above all else. Satan himself had tasked him with this goal, as he was busy manipulating war and destruction in other parts of the earth. Satan's grip tightened on the edge of the pool as he willed his clone to move faster, eager to reap the rewards of his sinister scheme.

How could he possibly conquer the world with such slow progress? It would take another two decades before the golden souls fully transformed into the black souls that would make up his massive army. He had already waited an eternity and wasn't willing to wait a single second more than he had to. This world was meant to be his, and he would stop at nothing to claim it. With a scowl of disgust, he turned away, snapping orders at the few demons who had the audacity to remain in his presence. His impatience was palpable as he demanded they deliver his urgent message to Natas, urging him to hasten his progress. He had no time to waste sitting around and waiting for his so-called 'brother' to get things moving. There were wars to wage and chaos to tend to, and he would not let anything, or anyone stand in his way. The air crackled with his anger as he strode off, leaving a trail of fire and brimstone in his wake.

The seasons changed, and the leaves turned from vibrant greens to fiery oranges. Shelley discovered an unexpected joy blossoming within her: she was pregnant. The news came as a whirlwind of emotions, both daunting and exhilarating, solidifying the bond between her and Nick even further. With their future taking shape before them, they decided to marry before Shelley's pregnancy became too visible.

Despite Shelley's initial shock, Nick was able to convince her to have a small ceremony at the courthouse instead of a traditional church wedding. When she asked why he didn't want to marry in his own church, he claimed that there were no other pastors available at such short notice.

They stood hand in hand, surrounded by the hushed anticipation of a new chapter beginning. They exchanged heartfelt vows, promising to build a life of love and mutual respect. The small setting of the ceremony reflected the deep, personal connection they shared - a testament to their journey from mere acquaintances to devoted lovers, soon-to-be parents.

The joyous celebration of Nick and Shelley's union spread like wildfire amongst the devoted followers of the Church of Ancient Souls. From every corner of the city, devotees erupted in unrestrained excitement, throwing parties and singing praises with their voices reaching a fever pitch, their bodies swayed to the infectious beat of drums. The air was alive with the sounds of laughter and joy, mingling with the aroma of spicy foods... Gleaming faces and outstretched hands joined together in celebration of this massive milestone- each one welcoming Shelley with open arms. To them, she was not just Nick's beloved wife but a symbol of their leader's enduring legacy, her presence solidifying their faith and devotion. The air was electric with unity as the church community came together to celebrate this sacred union.

Nick meticulously ensured that Shelley remained unaware of the church's true demonic nature. To her, he was a devoted pastor leading a community of faithful believers; she loved that his followers called him 'Lord'. She admired his dedication and the reverence he commanded from his followers, never suspecting the dark truths lurking beneath the surface. She had no idea that she had married a man who shared his body with the soul of Satan's clone.

Shelley embraced her new role, participating in church activities and mingling with the congregation, her heart full of love and hope for their shared future.

The grand halls of the Glitz were ablaze with a dazzling display of lights, sparkling and shimmering in every corner. The air was alive with the tinkling notes of laughter and the harmonious melodies of live music. Shelley, the mastermind behind it all, had come up with the idea to throw lavish parties each time a new church was opened, celebrating their expansion and success. Invitations had been sent out to an eclectic mix of high-ranking politicians, esteemed actors, popular rock stars, and devoted members of the congregation. They were encouraged to bring a 'plus one' as a way to further spread the Church's influence.

This first grand event at the luxurious Glitz Hotel in New York was a celebration two years after the opening of the very first church. The extravagant party was a resounding success, with music and laughter filling the air as guests danced and mingled. As the night went on, new friendships were formed, and old ones were strengthened, creating a sense of camaraderie and joy throughout the room. The glittering lights and lavish decorations added to the undeniable charm of the evening, making it an unforgettable experience for all who attended.

Kenny Reeves, the world-renowned actor with a commanding presence and glowing white aura, arrived at the Glitz accompanied by fellow A-list actors Tom Suise and John Revolva. The large, imposing security guards stood at the entrance, barring anyone from entering without authorization. Despite being invited by Tom and John, this guest was refused entry, and there was quite a commotion at the front door of the prestigious venue. A sense of intrigue pulled at Shelley as she made her way towards the entrance, wondering what could have caused such a scene. She caught sight of Kenny Reeves from a distance, getting back into his sleek white car and speeding away. He had seen enough and promptly left, announcing that the event was not for him.

John Revolva and Tom Suise's raised voices filled the air. Their anger was palpable, directed at the group of imposing men who stood resolute in their decision to deny entry to their friend. The atmosphere crackled with tension as the guests tried to understand what had caused this sudden disturbance. Shelley soon arrived on the scene like a ray of sunshine. Her soothing words and charming demeanour quickly smoothed over the situation, and when Lord Nick himself appeared- peace was restored, and the disruption was soon forgotten amidst the laughter and chatter of the guests.

But this was not an isolated incident for Lord Nick.

The renowned rockstar, Jon Golli, radiating a bright white aura, had also arrived at the door earlier in the evening. However, before any of the goons could take action, he abruptly turned away, feeling intense discomfort as he neared the entrance. Few individuals were even aware of his presence.

And as the Church grew in popularity, so did its flock of wealthy and prestigious followers, many of whom seemed to radiate a dark aura. Some had travelled from afar, desperate to reclaim their former fame, and saw Lord Nick as their potential saviour. Others sought his guidance to jumpstart their careers and gain favour in the public eye. But amidst all the glitz and glamour, there was a palpable sense of desperation, ambition, and blind faith that drew these individuals into the fold. Little did they know, they were unknowingly surrendering their souls to the darker forces at play within the Church.

Shelley basked in the luxuries of her new life as Mrs. Nicholas Green and her newfound status as one of society's elite. Though she had never dreamt of belonging to this exclusive group, she fit in seamlessly.

As they navigated their new life together, Shelley's blissful ignorance allowed her to see only the love and devotion she believed was at the heart of the church. She remained oblivious to the dark and powerful forces at play, and Nick intended to keep it that way, no matter the cost.

She didn't seem to pick up on the change in Nick's voice when he preached or when his henchmen referred to him as "Natas" instead of "Lord Nick." She assumed it was just a nickname.

Nick took it upon himself to personally visit each potential site for his new churches. It wasn't that he lacked trust in his servants; he simply wanted to ensure that each location had the same unique ambiance. Essential features included the red stained-glass windows, boarded just enough to let some light filter through but no prying eyes, the polished mahogany of the wooden pews and floors, and the pristine white marbling of the altar. Nick could sense the energies of the old buildings long before any renovations began, and he relished the travel. Occasionally, Shelley accompanied him, much to the delight of the congregations, who were thrilled to see them both appear.

Shelley watched in awe as her husband 'healed' the sick children, completely unaware of the true nature of the soul switches taking place. The auras within the congregations had changed; there was now a rich tapestry of colours and dark souls, and Natas had earned widespread admiration. Only those with the darkest souls had any inkling of Nick's true nature.

***

The grand party at the Glitz Hotel was a distant memory as the second Church opened in Los Angeles. The air was alive with excitement and anticipation as guests arrived in luxury vehicles, eager to attend the prestigious event held at the luxurious Winton Hotel. Flashing cameras and adoring fans lined the red carpet, hoping to catch a glimpse of their favourite Hollywood stars. The venue itself was adorned with opulent decorations and lavish furnishings, creating an atmosphere of extravagance and wealth.

Shelley, heavily pregnant and glowing, beamed proudly at her husband as he gracefully worked the crowd with his charm and charisma. As they mingled with high society elites from all corners of the USA, it was clear that this was a who's who of Hollywood. Politicians like Bill Winton and Arnold Hore rubbed shoulders with business moguls like Mr. Rump while aspiring performers and starlets tried to make a name for themselves in the ruthless nature of the industry.

But beneath the glitz and glamour of the event, there was a dark undercurrent. Some attendees were already consumed by demons, while others were slowly being corrupted by their own dark deeds. The air was thick with the scent of expensive perfumes and cheap ambitions, intertwining in a chaotic dance under the glittering lights that cast deceptive shadows on the faces of the attendees.

Amidst the powerful figures moving around her like predators in a jungle, a young starling, Kate Studson, stood at the edge of the room with a mixture of awe and fear in her eyes. She had been promised by her co-star Casey Leflick that this event would launch her career, but he had deserted her once they entered the venue. Now she watched him trying to get close to the host, Lord Nick, the enigmatic host of the night who seemed to hold all the power. Kate had heard of Lord Nick but had yet to meet him, and she was feeling nervous as the night went on. As rumours of satanic healings and unsavoury deals whispered through the room, mingling with clinking glasses and laughter, a sense of tension hung in the air. Kate couldn't shake off the growing unease inside her, a primal instinct urging her to escape before it was too late. Mr. Rump's cold eyes lingered on her for a moment too long, and she felt a chill run down her spine. She had seen other well-known figures, like talk show host Opal Hinfrey and actresses Angelina Hollie and Jerry Minefield, turning away from this mysterious place. And yet, she couldn't decipher its true nature. Why were these superstars being denied entry? The answer eluded her, as only Lord Nick and his trusted cohorts had the ability to see the glowing auras of their guests.

The night seemed to stretch on endlessly, filled with a sense of unease that refused to dissipate. Finally, Casey made his way over to her and grabbed her by the hand, "I'll introduce you to Lord Nick," he said, his voice barely audible over the chatter and music. Reluctantly, she followed him through the crowded party, her heart pounding in her chest. As they got closer, Lord Nick turned, and their eyes locked. He smiled a charming smile, but something about it sent shivers down her spine. And then it hit her. That smile, that evil smile- she had seen it before in primary school, where Nicholas Green had somehow managed to make her fall over and smash her teeth and jaw on the pavement. Her eyes widened in disbelief as the memories flooded back. She pulled her hand free from Casey's grip and turned to run through the crowd, desperate to escape the looming presence of Nicholas Green. She finally burst out of the doors, gasping for breath as she leaned against a nearby building. But even as she tried to calm herself, she couldn't shake off the lingering feeling that something dark and foreboding was lurking beneath the shiny facade of Hollywood- and his name was Nicholas Green. With a wave of relief washing over her, she hailed a cab and made her escape from the dangerous party and its predatory host.

***

Shortly after arriving back home to New York, Shelley felt the first contractions of labour, and as the gentle rays of the rising sun cast a warm glow over the summer morning, baby Dabria Green, surrounded by a golden aura with a tinge of orange, took his first breath in the world. In a serene and uncomplicated birth, Shelley smiled with pure exhaustion but also with unbridled elation as she cradled her newborn son. By her side stood Nick, his heart overflowing with love and pride for both his wife and child. Nick studied his newborn's aura and then shrugged it off- after all, it was still golden. The doctor declared the mother and baby healthy and thriving, as they left the hospital to embark on their new journey together.

With unwavering eagerness, Nick wasted no time in introducing Dabria to his congregation at the next service. The walls of the church reverberated with applause and cheers as Nick shared the news of his son's arrival and revealed his powerful name - Dabria, a name rich in meaning as "Angel of Death," a symbol of strength to those who knew its true significance. With Natas living within him, he felt a sense of invincibility, knowing he would go to any lengths to keep them safe.

SIX

Shane O'Donahue was a young and ambitious lawyer with hazel green eyes and an air of determined confidence. He had always been drawn to the mystique of New Orleans. The city, with its rich history and diverse culture, was the perfect place for him to start his career in criminal law.

Despite his reservations about representing big-time criminals, Shane couldn't resist the allure of the Big Easy. He had been offered a position at a prestigious firm in the heart of the French Quarter - and he eagerly accepted, eager to make a name for himself in a city known for its colourful characters and complex legal system.

The decision to move over two years ago proved to be the best he ever made. It was there that he first laid eyes on Bonnie, the stunning daughter of the owner of the law firm where he now worked. They had fallen head over heels for each other in a matter of weeks. He had always been a hit with women, but Bonnie was something else entirely - her beauty could easily grace the pages of a fashion magazine.

Although she was not at the top of her class, her unyielding love and support more than compensated for it. On the other hand, he had always excelled academically in university, thanks to his inherent intelligence and knack for balancing parties with studying. But now, he found himself navigating a complex world where the lines between right and wrong were blurred. He couldn't help but draw parallels to his university days, juggling assignments and social events, only this time with Bonnie by his side. With her unwavering companionship, he felt unshakably confident in facing whatever challenges may come their way. It was like having a constant anchor to keep him grounded amidst the unpredictable tides of life.

Determined to excel in his role, Shane's unwavering focus and relentless work ethic drove him to succeed. Nothing could stand in the way of his ambitions- he put in countless hours and took on as many clients as possible, knowing they were the key to impressing

Bonnie's father and making a name for himself at Righteous Resolutions- Criminal Lawyers.

The bustling city of New Orleans had become his new home, and he couldn't be happier with how his life had turned out.

Rising quickly through the ranks at the prestigious law firm, Shane's dedication and drive earned him a partnership within a short period of time. He gazed out at the vibrant streets below from his office window, feeling a sense of fulfillment and contentment. This was exactly where he was meant to be.

But it wasn't just his career that flourished in New Orleans - within months of meeting, Shane and Bonnie fell deeply in love and were soon married in a lavish ceremony surrounded by loved ones. As they settled into their roles as husband and wife, he was grateful for all the pieces that had fallen into place for him. And now, with their first child on the way, he eagerly awaited the arrival of the little bundle of joy.

He sat in his office between client meetings. He basked in the glow of his successes-he felt like he was on top of the world. Living in one of the most vibrant cities in America with a successful career and an adoring wife by his side, nothing could bring him down from this high.

The calming sense of contentment that washed over him quickly extinguished as his trusted secretary, Linda, burst into the room. The clicking of her heels echoed off the walls, a stark contrast to the peaceful silence just moments before. She carried with her a wave of urgency and concern; her voice trembled as she delivered the news about strange fires ravaging law firms in New York City. Shane couldn't believe what he was hearing. The thought of such destruction hitting so close to home sent shivers down his spine, shaking the very foundation of his perfect world.

On his computer screen, the news report showed buildings engulfed in flames and smoke billowing into the sky. The footage showed people running in panic, smoke billowing from the buildings, and firefighters battling the blazes.

He sat glued to the news broadcasting on every station, the images flickering and dancing before him like a twisted ballet of destruction and chaos, detailing the dreadful fires that had ravaged five of New York's top law firms. Without tearing his eyes from the screen, he dialled his friend Tommy Perkins on his mobile.

"Are you seeing this?" Tommy answered, clearly also engrossed in the news. "Anyone we know in those fires?"

"Maybe. A lot of people we were at uni with stayed in New York. The only one I'm sure of was Shelley Knights—she worked at McAdam's. But they haven't released any names of the casualties yet," Shane replied.

"Fuck—how can those fires not be related?" Tommy queried, disbelief lacing his voice.

"I know," Shane said solemnly.

After a few long minutes of heavy silence, the two sat on opposite ends of the phone, both reeling from the devastating news of the fires. Shane struggled to gather his thoughts before finally speaking up.

"I was actually calling to see if you and Kath wanted to make the trip down on Saturday. I know it's a bit of a drive from Baton Rouge, but Bonnie has her heart set on getting everyone together. We can set up the spare room for you if you'd like." He paused, knowing that his friend needed time to process before making a decision.

"She's also hoping Eddie and his wife...what's her name again? Ah yes, Alison...can join us as well." The thought of all their friends gathering together brought a glimmer of hope in the midst of such tragedy.

"Check with Kath and get back to me by tomorrow- I gotta go— I have another call, probably work. I'll flick out an email and see if Ed's free too." Shane hung up and sat staring at the TV a bit longer, letting the phone on his desk ring. Jesus, what a shock—all those dead lawyers in New York.

As the gravity of the tragedy sank in, a thought began to take shape. While the loss of life was tragic, it also presented a unique professional opportunity. Perhaps he could open an office in New York and bring the whole gang together. Out of this terrible disaster, he could see a chance for growth. If they could get together for the BBQ Bonnie had planned, maybe they could toss the idea around. Shane's mind raced with possibilities as he considered the future.

At last, Shane answered the call from his desk phone. It was Linda, his secretary, informing him that Mr. Robinson was on line two and reminding him that Bonnie, his wife (as if he needed reminding), had called to confirm the BBQ on Saturday. While he listened to Linda's updates and muttered his acknowledgments, he typed out a quick email to his buddies with the subject line, "Saturday 14th, BBQ 7 pm." The email reiterated what he had already told Tommy, and he sent it off just as Linda finished speaking.

Shane hung up and pressed the number two on his phone keypad to take the call from his client, Mr. Robinson. The man had been accused— and probably was guilty—of assaulting his partner. Despite his immense wealth and reputation as a real estate mogul in the bustling city of New Orleans, Mr. Robinson was infamous for his short temper. By the time Shane answered, Mr. Robinson was frantic. "She's died," he blurted out. "The bitch has died, and now the cops are blaming me!"

Well, that certainly escalated quickly, Shane thought. Yesterday, Mr. Robinson had contacted him about representing him, claiming it was just a small argument. Now, he was saying she had died. "We can't discuss this over the phone, Mr. Robinson. You'll need to book an appointment with Linda and come in to discuss it. Have the police been to see you?"

"Not yet," Mr. Robinson grunted.

"Don't talk to them without me being present," Shane advised. He transferred the call back to Linda and sat back in his chair, marvelling at how quickly things could change. It must've been one hell of an argument if Mrs. Robinson had died from it, he mused.

Shane's thoughts drifted back to the possibility of returning to New York and setting up a business with his best friends. Opportunities like this didn't come along every day, he realized. 'O'Donahue, Sampson, and Perkins Law Firm' had a nice ring to it, he thought. His name would, of course, be first; the order of the other two didn't matter to him— they could fight over it or draw straws if need be.

Initially, he hadn't been particularly excited about Saturday's BBQ. Catching up with old friends was always nice, but the presence of the wives often made things a bit mundane. Now, however, he was genuinely looking forward to it. Secrets would be shared once the women were out of earshot, and together, the three best friends could forge a plan to expand to New York. The coming days were filled with potential and excitement, and Shane couldn't wait to dive in.

Eddie Sampson was the only one of the three who had stayed in New York. He had settled down, marrying Alison, and they now had a one-year-old daughter, Mia. Eddie worked for Morley and Sons, a prestigious family law firm, and had quickly made a name for himself as one of the best in the field. Divorce cases came through the door every day, and he relished the opportunity to take a slice of the settlement pie.

Alison, on the other hand, was a successful real estate agent for Carey Group, specializing in selling million-dollar apartments and homes across New York. She had a natural flair for staging and styling properties to fetch the best prices. Together, they had amassed a significant fortune, becoming millionaires in their own right. Their lives were a whirlwind of professional success, and little Mia was predominantly cared for by a live-in nanny, rarely seeing her busy parents.

Eddie chuckled when he received Shane's email about the BBQ in New Orleans. The idea of jetting off for a casual get-together seemed laughable amidst their hectic schedules. Life had become so demanding that he and Alison had to meticulously plan quality time to spend as a family. There was no way they could make it to New Orleans for a BBQ.

Eddie quickly replied to Shane's email, politely declining the invitation. He wished them all a wonderful night and added, "Have a drink for me." Eddie closed his laptop and leaned back in his chair, a satisfied smile curling his lips. He relished his lavish lifestyle and had no qualms about the choices he'd made. From his wonderful marriage and luxurious Manhattan apartment to the significant bank balance, he felt complete. Life was good, and while he had fond memories of the past, he knew he wouldn't trade his current life for anything else.

As he thought about the upcoming weekend, he made a mental note to schedule some time for a family outing. Success tasted even sweeter when balanced against the occasional touch of normalcy, and Eddie enjoyed every bit of his dual life. He was right where he wanted to be, savouring every luxury New York had to offer.

Shane was getting ready to leave the office at 7 pm on Friday the 13th of March, when he got a call from NOPD. They had Mr Robinson in for questioning, and he wasn't saying a word without his attorney, so he jumped into his car and drove the short distance to the police headquarters on South Broad Street, he parked his car and went inside, briefly talked to an officer at the reception desk and was escorted back to an interrogation room where his client Mr Robinson was being held.

"Je-SUS," he cursed when Shane entered the room, "I thought you would never get here. Can we talk in here, or are they listening?"

"I think we're all good Mr Robinson" Shane said, "what have you told them?"

"Nothing – I swear, from the moment they cuffed me and threw me into the back seat of the cruiser, "I just repeated I want my lawyer."

"Good, good- now tell me the whole story this time, Pete, and don't bullshit me; I need to know how I can get you out of here, and bullshit washes off," Shane said.

Pete Robinson was a man in his sixties, and he preferred to be addressed as Mr. Robinson unless spoken to by a friend. This time, he let it slide as Shane had called him Pete; after all, Shane was trying to save his bacon.

Pete launched into his story, his voice trembling with tension. "We had indulged in a few drinks during dinner - just a couple of glasses of wine with the meal and maybe a few more at the bar. We were meeting with potential clients to discuss the sale of an old church near the cathedral down off Jackson Square. The people we talked to seemed important, like high flyers, but there was something eerie about them. It was as if dark shadows swirled around them all night, casting a foreboding feeling over the conversation. I tried to brush it off as just the lighting in the place, but there was definitely something off about them.

The price they were offering for the church was astronomical, thanks to its prime location. The man leading the deal, Nick - he claimed to be a Lord - didn't seem bothered by the cost."

Pete's voice caught in his throat as he continued, the memories still fresh and haunting. "My wife, who was clearly intoxicated, went on and on, ranting about the outrageous cost of the property - and just when it seemed like she couldn't stop talking, she dropped the bomb that she didn't even think this guy was actually a real Lord, then she leaned over and whispered to the other man's wife - not very quietly either - that she heard he was some kind of devil worshipper." Pete shuddered, remembering the look on Shelley's face when his wife uttered those words.

"The woman, Shelley, looked at her like she had gone mad," he went on, his voice trembling. "But I swear Nick shot her a look, and for a split second, his eyes turned red. I thought he was going to strangle her right then and there, but he just smiled at his wife and acted like he didn't hear anything."

Pete's hands shook as he recalled the events of that evening. "Next thing I know, my wife's lips are pursed tightly together- like a duck- and she looks absolutely terrified." He could still see the fear in her eyes, the way her body stiffened with each passing moment.

"I made up an excuse to leave and asked the valet to bring our car around," Pete said, his voice dropping lower. "As we got inside, I noticed something strange - a huge shadow seemed to get into the backseat with us. It hovered over my wife the entire drive home."

Shane leaned in closer, intrigued by the story. "What did you do?"

"I couldn't take my eyes off the shadow," Pete replied, his tone becoming more hushed and tense. "It seemed fixated on my wife... like it wanted something from her. I tried to ignore it- thought it was a figment of my imagination- but now..." He shuddered at the thought.

"And your wife? Did she say anything?" Shane pressed.

"No," Pete said with a heavy sigh. "She didn't speak a single word during the whole trip. Just sat there with her lips pursed tight."

Shane leaned in, curiosity piqued. "Did the argument carry on once you got back home?" Pete's face darkened as he shook his head. "No, my wife didn't utter a single word during the drive.

I ranted and raved about everything that had happened that night all the way home. For the first time in our marriage, she didn't interrupt me or offer her own opinions. I have to admit - It was a refreshing change,but when we arrived at our destination, she just sat there in the car, her eyes were wide, and her lips pursed tightly." He paused, taking a deep breath before continuing his story. The tension in the air was palpable as they both waited for him to speak again.

"I began to question whether the shadow was real or just my imagination," he spoke with hesitation. "So, I decided to go inside and let her have some time alone, assuming she must be giving me the silent treatment- for what reason, fuck knows. I wasn't the one who said anything inappropriate. I poured myself a whisky and waited for her. After about thirty minutes, I went back to the car to see what was holding her up."

"And?" Shane prompted, leaning in even closer.

Pete's voice trembled as he went on. "She was just sitting there, in the exact same position. I opened her door, and she didn't budge. I reached for her, and she was as stiff as a statue... Her eyes were wide open," he said in a hushed tone.

"But she wasn't blinking... and her mouth, it was still in that weird, pursed position - like a duck bill, you know? But she was still breathing then, I swear."

Pete's voice trembled as he recalled the rest of that horrifying night. "As I pulled her out of the car, she slipped from my grasp and hit her head on the concrete. There was so much blood..." He trailed off, unable to continue for a moment.

"But she was still breathing," Shane urged him on.

Pete nodded shakily. "Her eyes looked right at me, and she made this funny, muffled noise. I panicked and called an ambulance, but when the police showed up, they were hell-bent on domestic violence. They thought I had abused her, but I swear I never hit my wife... not like that." His voice broke, and he fell silent as tears welled in his eyes and overflowed down his cheeks.

He rubbed his temples. "Pete, this sounds...unbelievable. Are you sure you didn't have more than a couple of drinks?"

"Look, I know it sounds insane, but I'm not making this up. This Nick guy... he was a Lord of something, surrounded by half a dozen goons who didn't eat or drink; they just watched. One of them kept coming up and whispering things in his ear. He seemed to be the main goon and called him 'Lord' all night. There was something off about him—the guy, Lord Nick. I swear, his eyes flashed red when she made that comment," Pete said, desperation creeping into his voice.

Shane took a deep breath. "Alright, let's focus.

Pete nodded, though his eyes betrayed his anxiety. "What do we do now?"

"We're going to get you through this interrogation. I'll start looking into this Nick character to see if there's anything we can use in your defence. But for now, let's focus on keeping you from saying anything that could incriminate you," he said, steeling himself for what lay ahead.

Shane knocked on the door, signalling the officer outside. "We're ready," he said.

The officer escorted them to the interview room, where the harsh

Green.

"What the actual fuck?" he muttered to himself, unable to process what he was seeing. There they were, the same Nicholas Green, the sociopathic idiot from his university days, now parading around with a lordly title. And standing beside him was none other than THE Shelley Knights.

He blinked several times, but the image didn't change. The disbelief was overwhelming; he could hardly wrap his mind around this improbable turn of events. Nicholas Green, the same loser he had tormented at university, now styled as 'Lord Nicholas Green'? And Shelley, the untouchable beauty, by his side? It was too surreal to fathom.

He was both shocked and excited—he couldn't wait to share this outrageous revelation with his friends. He pictured the looks on their faces when they found out. Tonight, at least, he would be seeing Tommy, and maybe they could call Ed and loop him in on the unbelievable news. No one was going to believe this.

Swiftly, Shane saved the link to the Church of Ancient Souls website and emailed it to himself for easy access later. He knew that showing his friends the photograph of Lord Nicholas Green and Shelley Knights would be the highlight of their evening. Rubbing his hands together with anticipation, he savoured the thought of their collective disbelief and laughter.

Before heading home to fire up the BBQ, he made a critical call to the hospital. He needed to speak with the coroner who had performed the autopsy on Mrs. Robinson. The news was grim and did not bode well for Pete. According to the coroner, Mrs. Robinson had been strangled before falling from the car and hitting her head on the concrete.

Although she was still alive when the ambulance transported her to the hospital, her larynx had been crushed. She was brain-dead long before succumbing to her injuries.

The coroner clarified that while the fall might have been accidental, the crushed larynx was unequivocally a result of strangulation. This was neither accidental nor incidental. In his final assessment, the coroner concluded that Mrs. Caroline Robinson had been murdered.

Tommy and Kath drove the eighty-two miles from Baton Rouge to New Orleans in just over two hours, not too bad considering the heavy traffic on the way out. Tommy held Kath's hand for most of the drive, and Kath played DJ, picking songs from Tommy's cd collection, she turned up the sound to sing along for some of the bangers and they chatted easily in between. It was apparent they had only been dating a few months by the constant touching. The moment they arrived at Shane and Bonnie's beautiful old-plantation style home, they were whisked away separately by the hosts. Shane was apologetic as he whisked his buddy Tommy away, straight into his den, making an excuse that they had urgent matters to discuss about the case he was working on, and Bonnie was happy to have Kath all to herself. She couldn't wait to catch her up on all the details of her pregnancy and the upcoming birth of her baby, which was just five short weeks away. It had been months since they had seen each other and although they didn't know each other all that well, they were fast becoming good friends. Kath took in every detail of Bonnies radiant glow, from her rounded belly to her glowing complexion. She was filled with excitement for her new friend's journey into motherhood.

Shane poured two glasses of dark, amber liquid for himself and Tommy, he couldn't contain his excitement any longer. He launched into a detailed account of what he had discovered about Nicholas Green and Shelley Knight, pulling up the website for the mysterious Church they were affiliated with. Both men sat with their jaws agape as they delved deeper into the twisted world of these two individuals. Shane then revealed his plan to interview him about the evening Mrs. Robinson died, hoping to uncover some new information.

They mulled over the possibility that the police had already interrogated Green but ultimately resolved to take matters into their own hands. They would start by contacting their mutual friend Eddie hoping that perhaps Ed could delve deeper into the Church before Shane made his way to New York. After all, Eddie still lived in the city and may have connections or information that could aid their investigation.

Shane dialled Eddie's number, his fingers tapping anxiously on the screen. The phone rang and rang, but no one picked up.

The room was filled with a sense of anticipation and determination as they prepared to unravel the mysteries surrounding Lord Nicholas Green and Shelley Knights.

After failing to reach Ed, the conversation turned to Shane's impending case and the mysterious shadows. Tommy's mind wandered back to that night in university when Ed had shared a terrifying tale. The memory sent a chill down his spine, but he quickly shook it off when they were interrupted by the women joining them in the den. Bonnie, full of energy and excitement, eagerly ushered everyone outside, where she couldn't wait to start up the BBQ.

The warm summer sun began to set, so they all made their way out into the backyard. The tall trees swayed gently in the breeze, casting dappled shadows on the well-manicured lawn. The air was filled with the sweet fragrance of blooming flowers and freshly cut grass.

Shane expertly tended to the sizzling meats on the bbq, sending mouth- watering scents wafting through the air. Once the cooking was done, the group gathered around a cozy outdoor seating area illuminated by twinkling fairy lights strung up among the branches of nearby trees. As they sipped on chilled glasses of wine and savoured bites of delicious food, their easy laughter and chatter filled the warm summer night.

The guys grinned as they shared stories from their younger, wilder days while Bonnie and Kath regaled them with tales of their travels and adventures. Their laughter echoed through the night, mingling with the chirping of crickets and distant sounds of traffic. And when Nicholas Green's name came up, a hush fell over the group as Bonnie and Kath recounted what they had heard about his miraculous healing abilities that had touched so many lives around the world.

Shane's eyebrows shot up in disbelief, Tommy's eyes widened in shock. They exchanged glances, their expressions mirroring each other as they tried to process what they had just heard about Lord Nicholas Green.

Shane couldn't believe he and Tommy hadn't heard about it before, but Bonnie laughed and said that he never listened to her anyway.

***

The defendant, Mr. Robinson, appeared to have aged ten years since the last time Shane had seen him. His hair was dishevelled and thinning as if he had been pulling at it in distress. Deep bags under his eyes betrayed sleepless nights and anxiety. He anxiously wrung his hands together as the Judge read out the serious charges against him

– 2nd-degree murder. The bail amount, set at a staggering 1 million dollars, hung heavily over the courtroom like a dark cloud. Mr. Robinson's eyes darted nervously between the stern Judge and Shane, his lawyer. It seemed as though he was on the verge of breaking down and bursting into tears at any moment.

Shane placed a comforting hand on Mr. Robinson's trembling one, trying to soothe his nerves and prevent him from shattering completely. He couldn't imagine the bail being too difficult for the old man to come up with. The way he lived, surrounded by luxury and extravagance, made it seem that money was of little concern. He probably had a stack of cash ready to hand over at a moment's notice. The older man's grateful gaze met Shane's, filled with relief and vulnerability and expressing gratitude without words for being there in this moment of crisis. Shane felt a pang of guilt for his previous judgemental thoughts.

After ensuring Mr. Robinson had arrived safely at his home, Shane began to arrange for his own travel plans to New York. A quick search on the internet led him to discover that Nicholas Green was now living in luxury at none other than the Glitz Hotel. He marvelled at how effortlessly he could access information online, making his job as a private investigator so much easier. He could have simply called and arranged a meeting with Nick over the phone, but he was intrigued by the unexpected twist in Nick's life - from studying law to becoming a Lord and a preacher. A surprise visit seemed like the best option to get some answers.

With a dull thud, his feet hit the ground in New York City just after 11 am. He had been hoping for an earlier flight, eager to arrive and see Nick right away. However, there were no early flights available, much to his disappointment. Aided by the bustling city sounds and sights, he hopped into a yellow taxi and directed the driver to his hotel - nothing as luxurious as the Glitz hotel, but still a very nice place called The Aarkway. It was conveniently located within walking distance to the Glitz.

Deciding to wait until the morning to visit Nick, he dialled Eddie's number on his way. Eddie hadn't returned any of his calls in the last week, which wasn't entirely unusual, but Shane had some big news to share with him and wondered if Eddie had heard about Lord Nick.

Eddie answered after a few rings. "Sorry I didn't get around to calling you back, bud. I've been busy," he said bluntly. Straightforwardness was one of Eddie's greatest qualities.

"It's all good, Ed. I just landed in the Big Apple and was hoping we could catch up over lunch or drinks somewhere. I'm staying at The Aarkway on Central Park street," Shane invited.

"Oh wow, yes definitely. Let's see…I'll have to juggle some appointments around but how about 2pm? I'll come to you since I have an appointment in that area anyway," Eddie replied before hanging up.

Shane was already two drinks deep, comfortably perched on a stool at the polished wooden bar, when Eddie finally arrived. As always, they greeted each other with a hearty slap on the back followed by a firm handshake. The clasp lingered for a moment longer than usual, both men feeling a twinge of emotion at their long-awaited reunion. It had been over a year since Shane's wedding, the last time they had seen each other. Now, as grown men with families and successful careers, it seemed that their once inseparable friendship had taken a backseat.

"Barkeep, my friend will have a whisky, neat," Shane called out to the bartender who promptly poured out the amber liquid into a pristine glass. The atmosphere in the bar was subdued, with only a few scattered groups occupying tables and booths. It was after the lunch rush and before the dinner crowd, and midweek blues keeping most people away. The few patrons present all seemed to be conducting business or discussing deals, their voices hushed and serious.

The two men moved to a dimly lit corner of the bar; Shane lowered his voice to a hushed tone. He confided in Eddie about the impending murder case he was working on. Criminal law was not new to him, he'd been working in the field for a couple of years now, but this one had certainly gripped his attention. He relayed the details passed on to him by the accused Mr. Robinson - from the shadows that loomed over their dinner conversation to the one that Mr. Robinson claimed ended his wife's life. But it wasn't just about Mr. Robinson and his deceased wife- he dropped a major bombshell about Nicholas Green, now apparently a prominent figure in society, and an even bigger revelation about Shelley Knights, now known as Mrs. Shelley Green. The weight of the news settled heavily between them, and they sat in stunned silence for a moment. Shane let his friend process the information before delving into the reason he was in New York: to interview Nicholas Green, also known as Lord Nick.

Eddie sat in silence, his mind swirling with the rumours he had heard about the Church of Ancient Souls and its enigmatic leader, Lord Nick. The new religious movement seemed to have taken New York and the world by storm, but Eddie had paid little attention to social pages or religious matters, he had not realised who Lord Nick actually was until now. He had heard whispers of miraculous healings and alleged connections to Satanism, but it all sounded absurd to him. Now, it was starting to come together.

Now, as Shane mentioned possibly getting involved with this controversial figure, a knot formed in Eddie's stomach.

The memories flooded back to him. The way they had treated Nick - with disdain, and the rumours that followed him around him like a dark cloud. Some believed he was cursed, others whispered about him being a potential murderer. And then there was the incident where he had suspended him off the ground, shadowy tendrils wrapping around him as Nick lay on his bed with a sinister grin and threatened to toss him out of the window. It was a memory that he had pushed deep down, but it resurfaced now.

He couldn't help but question Shane's judgment in reconnecting with someone who had proven themselves capable of such frightening displays. He knew that getting involved with Nick was downright dangerous and he had tried to caution Shane against it.

"I don't think it's a good idea," Eddie finally spoke up, his discomfort palpable. Ever since Shane mentioned Nick's name, a sense of unease had settled over him, causing the hairs on the back of his neck to stand on end. But Shane brushed off his concerns, insisting that Lord Nick was just a phony, desperate for followers after failing as a lawyer.

"He's always been a bit of a weirdo, hasn't he?" Shane laughed dismissively. "I bet he'll be scared shitless when he sees me." But Eddie couldn't shake the feeling that there was something more to this Lord Nick and his shadows - something dangerous and unsettling.

The clock struck 6 pm; Eddie excused himself and left for dinner with his family. Shane remained at the bar, nursing his fifth whisky of the day as he mulled over thoughts of Nicholas Green. The once quiet bar was now bustling with activity, the air thick with the smells of the evening's menu. Eddie's warnings about this man had shaken him - sure, he was eccentric, but could he also be dangerous? He started to question his own judgement. Memories of the rumours surrounding Nick during their time at university flooded his mind - was he really a killer? He never denied the accusations; in fact, he seemed to relish in the fear it caused among his peers. Maybe Eddie was right. Maybe he shouldn't go alone to meet with Lord Nick tomorrow morning. He decided to sleep on it, opting to retreat to his room and check in with Bonnie before ordering room service for dinner.

He approached the grand reception area of the luxurious Glitz hotel, his footsteps echoed off the marble floors. Politely, he asked the receptionist for Lord Nicholas Green's room number, trying to maintain a calm demeanour despite the nerves fluttering in his stomach. The receptionist raised an eyebrow and inquired if The Lord was expecting him. Shane stammered that he was an old friend in town and wanted to surprise him, but her sarcastic smile made it clear she had heard that excuse many times before.

"I'm sorry sir, but I cannot let you go up unannounced," she stated firmly. "I will call up to see if he will see you. May I have your name, please?"

"Ahh, Shane O'Donahue," he replied hesitantly, not wanting to reveal too much information. But then he reasoned that Nick would probably recognize him anyway when they met. Glancing at his watch, Shane saw it was now quarter past eight. Despite a restless night filled with nightmares of red-eyed shadows, he tried to convince himself they were just dreams. However, due to the lack of sleep, he had been up since 5am preparing a list of questions for Nick about their client, Mr Pete Robinson, and his late wife's suspicious death. With his notes in hand, Shane felt somewhat confident and pushed down any lingering apprehension.

He waited for the receptionist to make the call, feeling a little out of place in such opulent surroundings - the crystal chandeliers, the plush velvet drapes, the impeccably dressed guests mingling about. As he looked around, he felt a twinge of jealousy at those who were born into such luxury. After all, he had grown up in a well-to-do family, but nothing could compare to the excessive wealth flaunted by those who frequented this establishment. Quickly, he shook off these thoughts, determined to stay focused on the task at hand.

Nicholas Green burst out of the elevator and confidently strode towards the reception desk. His entourage of menacing goons fanned out around him, creating an almost impenetrable wall of muscle and power.

Shane had been waiting anxiously, fixated on the receptionist's every move as she chatted on the phone. Despite her back being turned to him, she seemed completely engrossed in conversation with whom he assumed was Lord Nick on the phone. Suddenly, Nick materialized beside him with a charming smile.

"Shane O'Donahue! It is so good to see you. It's been what, two years? Three?" Nick exclaimed, his voice overflowing with genuine excitement. Before Shane could even respond, Nick continued, "I must say, I was a little surprised to hear you had come to see me."

Shane finally found his voice and managed a simple greeting, "Hi, Nick. It's good to see you too." But inside, he was in shock. This was not the Nick he remembered. He looked somehow taller and more commanding than before, emanating an air of confidence that demanded attention. And he certainly didn't remember him being so strikingly handsome. But there he was - tall and ruggedly handsome, with piercing eyes that sparkled with a shade of purple, unlike anything Shane had ever seen before.

Caught up in the moment, he temporarily forgot why he had even come to see Nick in the first place.

Nick motioned for him to join him in the dining room, and he followed along. The waiters scurried over to lead them to their seats, placing Lord Nick at the head of a grandiose table with Shane seated next to him. As they settled in, Nick's charming smile and lively gestures captivated Shane as he shared stories of his thriving business ventures and recent dinner with the Robinsons. In fact, Shane hardly had a chance to ask any questions before Nick eagerly provided all the answers on his own.

The man seated next to him was a complete stranger, yet he bore the same face that had been the brunt of jokes throughout their Uni years.

The once weird and peculiar individual from their university days now exuded charm and wit, making it hard for him to keep up his guard. As Nick reminisced about their past antics, a part of him couldn't help but feel conflicted about the person who sat before him now.

"I suppose I've come out on top," Nick quipped, gesturing to his global renown and ultimate trump card - his marriage to Shelley. Shane couldn't help but marvel at how far his old classmate had risen since their time in school.

Shane's gaze swept around the room as the meeting came to an end, and he noticed the way the shadows seemed to dance and flicker against the walls. The soft glow of the chandeliers cast a warm light, highlighting the elegant furnishings and ornate wallpaper. But it was the shadows that caught his attention - they moved and swayed as if dancing to some invisible tune. There were no flickering lights like one would expect, yet the shadows continued their ethereal dance on the walls. Shane watched in wonder at this mysterious phenomenon, transfixed by its beauty and intrigued by its cause.

Lord Nick ended their meeting abruptly and rose from his seat. Shane's eyes scanned the room again, and he noticed the numerous 'goons' that had been standing guard, watching their every move. A knot formed in his stomach as he counted at least eight men following Nick back to the elevator. He couldn't shake off the unease that suddenly washed over him, knowing they had been under constant surveillance. As he sat, mind racing with thoughts of the recent meeting, it dawned on him that most of the questions had come from Nick himself. He now knew far more about Shane's personal life than he was comfortable with - where he lived, who he was married to, even asking about his past connections with Eddie and Tommy and their current whereabouts. It was almost as if Shane had been the one being interrogated- except he had willingly given up all the information without realizing it. Nick had been so relaxed and charming during their conversation that Shane hadn't even noticed how the tables had turned in a matter of minutes. In hindsight, he felt foolish for being caught off guard by Nick's smooth tactics.

On his flight home, his fingers flew across the keys of his open laptop as he frantically typed out all the information he could remember from his meeting with Nick. Despite their conversation appearing to be innocent and business-related, he couldn't shake off the uneasy feeling that had been nagging at him since he first met Lord Nick. The man seemed perfectly ordinary, just purchasing an old church like he had done in other parts of the world to grow his congregation. But something about him made Shane uncomfortable

- perhaps it was the way he was addressed as "Lord" or the fact that Shane never got around to asking how he obtained that title.

The unease continued to follow Shane even as he landed back in New Orleans. He found himself constantly looking over his shoulder, jumping at shadows and strange noises. The story Mr. Robinson had shared during their interview about a shadow following him and his wife home, possibly leading to her death, suddenly felt all too real. Not to mention the story Eddie had told him and Tommy back in Uni- And what about the rumours surrounding Lord Nicholas Green? Could they be true? Was he really a devil worshipper?

The plane descended towards the city; Shane felt like he had more questions than answers after his interview with Lord Nick. And now, as he made his way back home, he wondered if there was more to this encounter than meets the eye.

A rush of exhilaration coursed through Nick's body as he recalled the unexpected encounter with Shane O'Donahue. It was like winning the lottery, only better. Despite his busy life as a Lord, traveling and giving sermons to crowds of eager listeners and his 'healing' work, his thoughts often drifted towards finding Shane, Eddie, and Tommy.

And now, by some twist of fate, they had essentially fallen into his lap. The mere thought of getting revenge sent shivers of excitement down his spine.

Of course, he wasn't taking any chances this time. He had one of his trusted demons tailing Shane at all times - he wasn't about to let him slip away again. But what really fuelled his anticipation was the thought of witnessing their downfall - all three of them. This would be his greatest triumph yet, and he relished in the idea of being able to savour every moment of it. A sinister grin spread across his face as he basked in the thrill of imminent payback.

SEVEN

The days passed, and Bonnie's due date came and went; Shane's sense of foreboding only grew stronger. He couldn't shake the feeling that he was being watched, and at times, he could have sworn there was a mysterious shadow trailing him. He made an effort to hide his unease from Bonnie, not wanting to add to her worries during such an important time. After all, it was just a feeling.

In an effort to take his mind off things, he buried himself in work, dedicating even more time and effort than usual to preparing for the trial of Mr. Robinson.

Bonnie was filled with the unease of a different kind; her round belly stretched taut with the weight of a baby that was due three days ago. Despite her mother's reassurances that the baby had 'dropped', there were no indications that it was ready to make its grand entrance into the world. The pregnancy had been smooth sailing, and she and Shane meticulously prepared the nursery months in advance. Now, Bonnie sat in the cozy rocking chair, hands gently cradling her stomach as she softly spoke to her unborn child, pleading for them to come out into the world. Shane leaned against the doorway, admiring his wife's ethereal beauty. He never thought it possible for her to be more radiant than on their wedding day, but with their child growing inside her, she positively glowed. He could have watched her for hours, but he knew he had to leave soon for Mr. Robinsons' trial, which would begin in just a couple of hours.

He was exhausted and disheartened. He had poured countless hours into defending Mr. Robinson. But the odds were stacked against them- a guilty verdict seemed inevitable. Despite all his efforts, the only hope of avoiding a lifetime behind bars was to accept the plea deal that was on offer, a first-degree manslaughter conviction with a ten-year prison sentence. However, Mr. Robinson remained stubbornly insistent on his innocence and refused the offer, his steadfast belief in his own story unwavering.

To Shane, it seemed like an impossible task- how could he argue that a mere 'shadow' had committed the crime? He knew the jury would question Mr. Robinson's sanity, but still Mr Robinson insisted on telling them about the shadows that had been hovering around him and his wife at dinner with Lord Nick and the one that came with them- in their car - on their way home. It all sounded like the ramblings of a madman, and Shane struggled to find a way to incorporate it into his defence without jeopardizing their case. Of course, he could also try the insanity plea, but he was having trouble convincing his client to go with that either.

The weight of the situation pressed heavily on his shoulders- The stakes were high, and the evidence against them was strong, leaving little room for error or doubt.

Mr. Robinson's bizarre accusations lingered in his mind; he couldn't ignore the unsettling feeling that he too had been jumping at shadows. He couldn't deny what he had witnessed during his meeting with Lord Nick. But the logical part of him knew it would be impossible to prove anything without concrete evidence.

A heavy sigh escaped his lips as he contemplated his options, his eyes flickering over to Bonnie who sat on the rocker, her rounded stomach gently rising and falling with each breath.

He walked over and leaned in to give her a kiss goodbye, his hand tenderly caressing her bump. "See you soon, little guy," he whispered to their unborn baby.

Bonnie's face lit up with a mischievous grin. "She might be a girl, you know," she playfully teased. "I'll walk you to your car - it'll give me a chance to stretch my legs," she suggested, rising from her seat and leading him towards the front door. As they strolled towards his vehicle, Bonnie leaned in for one last kiss before he left for court. "Good luck with your case today," she said warmly, filled with admiration in her tone. "You look amazing! If I were the judge, I would definitely go with whatever you said." She laughed and took a step back as he backed out of the driveway. The sun was just starting to rise, casting a warm glow over the neighbourhood as he drove off toward what would undoubtedly be a challenging day in court.

He arrived at the downtown court and was met with a swarm of police cars blocking the road to his designated parking spot. Frustration flared within him - this was not what he needed on such an important morning. He rolled down his window and tried to reason with one of the officers, hoping they would let him through.

"Sorry, sir, you can't go that way," the officer responded.

He gritted his teeth. "I have a case this morning. I need to park here."

The officer's expression softened. "There's been a suicide, sir. An elderly gentleman jumped off the roof."

Shane's heart sank as he asked for a name. "A Mr Robinson- or Robson, if I remember correctly," the officer reluctantly confirmed. Shane's jaw dropped in disbelief, and he turned off his car engine. He sat there for a good five minutes in stunned silence. His mind raced as he thought about Mr. Robinson, their recent conversation, and how he had mentioned that the shadow was back and coming after him. Did the shadow cause him to jump, or did poor Mr. Robinson simply crack under the pressure?

After gathering his thoughts, he turned his car around and drove home with a heavy heart. He made a call to Bonnie on his way. The sound of her voice brought some comfort to his troubled mind. He recounted the details of his client's apparent suicide, still feeling uneasy about the suspicious death. The image of a shadow slipping into his car when he lowered the window to speak with the officer plagued him, but he forced it out of his mind, thinking how ridiculous it was- he focused instead on his beloved wife's attempts to comfort him.

He picked up the car phone and dialled Eddie's number, not expecting him to answer on the first ring. Eddie told him the suicide was all over the news, and Shane expressed how shocked he was and went on to share his unease and constant feeling of being watched since meeting Lord Nick, leaving out the suspicion of a shadow lurking in his car. There was a pause before Eddie responded with a warning: "Be careful," he cautioned. "I've heard some disturbing things about Lord Nick. - people are saying he's part of a devil's cult, and now, with two deaths surrounding him - both Mr. and Mrs. Robinson - maybe it's best for you to get away for a while. I believe the shadows are real." He went on without waiting for a reply. "I've been thinking a lot about that night at Uni when Nick never moved from his bed, but I tell you - something lifted me up and pinned me against the wall with its evil presence. It was enough for me to stay far away from Nicholas Green, and I think you should as well."

Shane and Eddie were saying their goodbyes when he turned down the familiar driveway to his house. Out of the corner of his eye, he caught sight of Bonnie rushing out to greet him. Her once petite frame, now carrying an enormous pregnant stomach, bounced along as she ran towards him with excitement.

In a split second, Shane's grip on the steering wheel loosened, and all control over the car slipped from his grasp. A shadow loomed over him, causing his heart to race even faster. Suddenly, a heavy weight pushed down on his arms and body as if trying to steer the car in a different direction. With wide eyes, he watched in horror as the vehicle careened off the driveway and onto the lush green lawn. Bonnie was standing frozen in her tracks, a look of pure terror etched on her face as she realized the impending danger heading towards her.

Desperately trying to hit the brakes and open his door at the same time, He could do nothing but scream as the car barrelled towards Bonnie, picking up speed with each passing second. The sound of shattering glass filled the air as the car collided with her body. She was thrown into the air like a ragdoll before landing with a sickening thud on the windshield and then tumbling over the top of the car. And finally, it came to a halt.

Shane's screams continued as he finally managed to free himself from the wrecked vehicle, and he raced towards Bonnie, cradling her head in his trembling hands. But it was too late. Her lifeless body lay sprawled in a pool of blood on the once pristine lawn, her eyes fixed on nothingness.

In that moment, Eddie's voice echoed through the phone, having heard everything unfold over their phone call. He could hear Shane's sobs as he wept uncontrollably, holding her still-warm body.

***

The sun was high in the sky, casting its warm rays across the desolate scene. He sat on the ground, his face streaked with tears while he frantically scanned the surroundings for any sign of help. Desperation filled him as he sobbed and cried out for someone to help him. In a moment of hopeful relief, he spotted a dark SUV parked across the road, its windows tinted and opaque, obscuring what was inside.

His heart skipped a beat as his gaze fell upon the vehicle, and he watched in horror as a shadow seemed to slither across the road. The window wound down, to allow the shadow to seep in. Panic filled his mind as he could have sworn he saw Nicholas Green sitting in the back seat with a twisted, unsettling grin on his face.

Before he could even process what he had seen, the window slid back up, and the SUV slowly drove away in eerie silence. He remained seated on the dewy lawn, cradling Bonnie in his arms, unsure if what had just happened was real or simply a figment of his imagination. The air hung heavy with a sense of danger and unease, like a storm brewing on the horizon, ready to unleash its fury at any moment.

Eddie's voice echoed through the phone, carrying a sense of frantic urgency as he called out to his friend. He could hear the crash and the screams as the accident happened and felt helpless, knowing he was too far away to do anything. After receiving no response, he reluctantly hung up and dialled the police, sending them to Shane's house to investigate what he could only imagine had happened. His heart raced as he tried calling Shane again but received no answer. In a state of panic, he called Tommy and filled him in on the situation as best he could. Without hesitation, Tommy agreed to drive down to New Orleans as soon as possible.

Eddie was well aware that he couldn't run away from his commitments- He had a crucial business meeting approaching, and with Allison out of town for work in the next two days, he needed to be home to care for their young daughter, Mia. Despite having a live-in housekeeper, they never left Mia alone without one of them at home during the evenings.

He promised to keep his phone nearby so Tommy could keep him informed.

The eerie silence of his phone hung over him like a dark cloud, casting a sense of foreboding that he couldn't shake.

He held it close all day as if it were a lifeline. He nearly blew a crucial meeting with a potential client, his mind consumed by the constant checking of his phone for any missed calls or messages. The client's irritation was palpable as Eddie struggled to focus on their discussion about millions of dollars. But in his mind, all he could think about was his friends, who were now strangely unreachable. As the evening wore on, a sense of foreboding settled over him like a heavy fog. Even when he finally arrived home and went to tuck his daughter Mia in, his mind couldn't stop racing with worry and fear.

Finally, as the clock struck midnight, his phone rang, making him jump. He answered with a shaky hand; his heart was pounding in his chest. "Shane was admitted to the hospital under police guard," Tommy said in a hushed voice. "He's a bloody mess, and Bonnie...and the baby..." His words trailed ofnsf as he struggled to hold back tears.

The silence on the other end of the line was heavy and Ed could almost feel the weight of it through the phone. "What happened?" he finally asked, his voice low and tense.

"Cops think he had some kind of breakdown. He says shadows took over his car, made him run her over," Tommy explained, "I don't know what to make of it all, Ed. This talk of shadows has been going on ever since he took that case with the Robinsons."

Ed listened intently, trying to make sense of it all. Memories flooded back of their time at university. "I think he's telling the truth," he said finally. "Nicholas Green is responsible for this- there are too many rumours about him being a Devil worshipper for there not to be any truth in this."

"Maybe," said Tommy thoughtfully, "Maybe he's got Satan on his side."

They talked for a while longer, both struggling to come to terms with the events that had unfolded. Before hanging up, Tommy mentioned having to get back to his girlfriend in Baton Rouge and promised to keep Ed updated.

As he walked back to his car, Tommy couldn't shake off the feeling of being watched. Strange shadows seemed to lurk around every corner now, and he felt a strange sense of unease. He tried to brush it off as his imagination playing tricks on him; all the talk about the shadows had made him jumpy, that was it - but deep down, he couldn't shake off a growing sense of dread.

Nicholas Green stood with a triumphant smirk on his face, revelling in the rush of emotions that flooded through him - relief, satisfaction, and a malicious glee that twisted his lips into a cruel grin.

After meticulously scheming and strategizing for years, Shane O'Donahue was finally getting his comeuppance for the torment he had inflicted upon him during their university days. Now, Shane's wife and unborn child were dead, and he would spend the rest of his days rotting away in a cold prison cell for their deaths. Though Nicholas had originally intended to kill Shane himself, this outcome was even better. Every day, Shane would suffer, knowing he was responsible for destroying his own family, and he would be behind bars for the rest of his miserable life. Nicholas basked in the satisfaction of revenge accomplished.

Upon arriving home, he immediately swept Shelley off her feet and whisked her away to a luxurious dinner followed by a leisurely stroll through Central Park- a romantic outing they hadn't indulged in since their early days of dating years ago. Shelley was under the impression that her beloved husband was celebrating their recent purchase of the quaint little church in New Orleans they had looked at only a few months before. Little did she know, he was mainly celebrating after witnessing Shane brutally run down his own heavily pregnant wife and not the signed paperwork on the church. Revenge was sweet for Nicholas, and he couldn't deny the satisfaction it brought him on this night, As the moon shone through the curtains, Nick lay intertwined with Shelley in the afterglow of their lovemaking. While she slept, he silently communicated with Natas, plotting the downfall of Tommy and Eddie.

A palpable electricity crackled between them as they plotted in the darkness. The air around them seemed to vibrate with an unspoken intensity, thick and heavy with deceit and malice.

Nick's heart raced with anticipation. He wanted to witness firsthand his enemies' demise. For him, seeing was always more satisfying than hearing about it after the fact.

A few days after Shane was admitted to the hospital, his heart heavy with grief and disbelief, he received news that only added to his turmoil. The detective who had interviewed him informed him that he was officially being charged with the murder of his beloved wife and unborn child. As if this wasn't enough to bear, he was also told that his car had been thoroughly examined and no mechanical issues were found.

His father-in-law called him as soon as he heard the news and, with disgust in his voice, told him he was wiping his hands of him. The man no longer saw him as a son-in-law but as a murderer. He blamed him for the death of his beloved daughter and her unborn child. And just like that, his whole life was ruined- Wife, Child and, career all gone. Even if he somehow managed to escape conviction for the crime, he knew he would never be able to find work as a lawyer in the USA again. Every door would be slammed shut, and every opportunity denied, all because of one tragic event that was not his fault.

The weight of this realization crushed down on him like a boulder, threatening to suffocate him under its immense pressure. The police had concluded that he either suffered a psychotic break or deliberately ran over his wife. It was a cruel blow, being treated as a criminal instead of a victim. In desperation, he requested that his trusted friend, Tommy, be his attorney, and, without hesitation, Tommy accepted the responsibility.

The prestigious firm Tommy worked for in Baton Rouge, aptly named the Baton Rouge Law Firm, was led by none other than Oliver Morrison - a shrewd and quick-witted man known for his no-nonsense approach. Despite being seen as a junior in the office due to his limited experience, Tommy's boss saw potential in him and was eager for Tommy to take on Shane's case. This was an opportunity for Tommy to prove himself in the cut-throat world of law, and Oliver had high hopes for his young protégé.

Tommy and Kath made plans to stay in the vibrant city of New Orleans during the looming trial, carefully packing their belongings into the car with uncertainty hanging over their heads. The weight of the situation weighed heavily on Tommy's shoulders; he still couldn't shake off the feeling that they were being watched. He warned Kath to stay close to him, his protective instincts kicking in. She smiled lovingly at him, not fully comprehending the danger they could be in.

Tommy had told her what he knew about the ominous shadows, but she found it hard to believe. On the contrary, Tommy was hyperaware of every shadow and movement, pulling over twice just as they headed off to investigate a perceived presence in the car with them before admitting it was probably just his mind playing tricks on him.

They travelled along Louisiana River Road in the mid-afternoons heat, following the winding path of the Mississippi, they made a planned detour to the opulent Country Club of Louisiana to pay a visit to Tommy's boss and bid their farewells. He had been incredibly supportive of Tommy's decision to represent his friend, and he was the one who had recommended they stay in New Orleans for the duration of the trial.

Eager to showcase the country club's prestige, Oliver warmly welcomed Tommy and Kath and offered to give them a tour. His eyes sparkled with hope as he envisioned them becoming members soon. He had taken a liking to young Tommy and saw great potential in him as a lawyer. As for Kath, he hoped she would join his wife's social circle, knowing how much they could benefit from a younger, bright, and charming addition to their group of friends.

As they entered the grand country club, Oliver greeted them with suave confidence. He reclined on a white leather armchair, sipping on a tumbler of whisky. Dressed in slate-gray wool trousers and a dark blue sweater, it was almost hard for Tommy to recognize him outside of the office and his usual business suit attire.

The club was abuzz with activity as it hosted a lavish function. Tommy and Kath couldn't help but feel underdressed compared to the well-dressed attendees. However, their worries were put to rest when Oliver offered to show them around the grounds.

With Oliver as their guide, they strolled around the immaculately manicured lawns of the club. Eventually, they reached a picturesque spot overlooking the Mississippi River. As they took in the serene view, Oliver suggested they stay for lunch before embarking on their long drive. The menu boasted exotic delicacies such as crabs and oysters, indicating just how prestigious this club truly was.

Tommy and Kath agreed to stay for lunch- there was no rush to reach New Orleans; the trial wasn't scheduled for a few more days. Oliver excused himself to inform the chef of their additional guests. Kath turned back to take in the beautiful view of the river, while Tommy watched as his boss made his way back to the clubhouse, it was then he noticed an ominous black SUV parked on the road nearby.

A chill ran down Tommy's spine as he turned to ask Kath if she had seen it, too. She had walked down to the edge of the river, and as she turned back and started walking toward him, his breath caught in his throat as a dark figure emerged from the water and slithered across the ground with chilling grace, resembling a human in a shadowy form. It moved swiftly, like a predator stalking its prey, and grabbed onto her ankles with an iron grip. She let out a blood-curdling scream as she fell and was dragged backward into the river. Her screams quickly turned into gurgles, panic surged through Tommy, and he lunged for her, grasping onto her arm in a desperate attempt to save her. The shadow pulled Kath under with a force that was too strong, and she slipped from Tommy's grasp, disappearing beneath the surface with a final gurgle of fear. Tommy tried desperately to find her in the murk until he felt cold hands on his shoulders, pushing him down into the frigid depths alongside Kath. He struggled against the unseen force, gasping for air and fighting to break free. He thrashed wildly in a panic, kicking and punching at the darkness surrounding him. But as the coldness of the water seeped into his bones, he felt himself losing consciousness, and he knew that Nicholas Green was watching from the backseat of the Black SUV.

The SUV raced away before anyone could even realize what had happened.

Oliver slowly began to realize that something was amiss when Tommy and Kath failed to show up for dinner. It had taken him over an hour to finally sound the alarm, and by then, it was too late. The glimmering waters of the Mississippi river lapped at the shore as if whispering secrets among themselves.

Police divers were called in, and after a painstaking search, they retrieved the lifeless bodies of Tommy Perkins and Kath Simmons from the depths below.

A maniacal grin spread across Nick's face as he checked another name off his list. Two down, and only one to go. The feeling of elation that coursed through him was almost overwhelming. He couldn't remember the last time he felt this ecstatic, aside from when he and Shelley had first gotten together. But this moment was even more satisfying than that. Natas would be pleased, of course, but that word didn't do justice to the intense joy Nick was experiencing. Once Eddie Sampson was taken care of, Nick could finally refocus on his true purpose - giving sermons and taking souls. He relished the thought of traveling more, as Natas had been urging him to for the last couple of years. It was time to expand his reach and meet with more of his followers around the world. With each new convert, Nick could feel his congregation growing stronger and his influence spreading further.

Eddie sat in his dimly lit den, the glow of the TV casting shadows on his face. Ever since Shane's wife's death and his subsequent arrest, he had been glued to the news, desperate for updates. He was in constant contact with Tommy, who was now representing Shane for his impending murder trial. Shane, on the other hand, was usually hard to reach, having sunk into a deep depression. But today, there was an eerie silence from Tommy. His absence was palpable, like a gaping hole, and now, according to the news- his lifeless body was recovered from the murky depths of the river.

In a state of shock, Eddie picked up the phone and dialled Shane's number. They both knew what this meant - their suspicions were confirmed. It had been Green all along. "My money's on Green," Eddie said bitterly when Shane finally picked up.

Shane's voice trembled on the other end of the line. "No doubt in my mind at all," he said. "He told me the shadows had been following him- said he was starting to think he'd lost his mind- But we both know it's real."

"I've been researching," Eddie said, his voice heavy with concern. "There's not much out there, but it does mention the shadows as part of a satanic cult on various web pages. I'm hesitant to dive too deep into it...it scares the hell out of me." As an afterthought, he added, "I have Allison and Mia to think of, too. And what about your trial now that Tommy's gone?" he sighed heavily. "I don't think there's any way to beat them either." He paused, considering his options. "Maybe we should move away? Me and Alison and Mia- Somewhere far where Lord Nick can't find us?"

Shane's reaction was immediate and desperate. "Eddie, you have to do it! Save yourself! I'm going to jail no matter what...there's no way I can prove my innocence - that I didn't kill Bonnie," he trailed off, his voice filled with anguish.

"Maybe you should consider changing your identities too," Shane suggested after taking a moment to collect.

Eddie's voice shook with raw emotion as he spoke. "That's not a simple fix- Christ, changing our names is just too much!" He ran a hand through his hair, the strands tangling between his fingers in frustration. "We have lives, jobs, and relationships here in New York. Just the thought of uprooting everything and starting over is overwhelming." His thoughts turned to Alison, his partner who had built a successful career and gained love and admiration from those around her. "I don't know how Alison will take this - she's set here, you know; she's established and respected. I just don't know if we can leave it all behind." Eddie's voice trailed off, his defeat palpable in the heavy silence that followed.

"Think about it, and let me know what you decide," Shane said softly. "Stay safe, my old friend." And with that, he hung up the phone.

With a sense of urgency and determination, Eddie frantically gathered his family's belongings and whisked them away to a small, coastal city tucked away in the charming country of Australia. The weight of the decision hung heavy on his mind as he left behind loved ones, friendships, and successful careers that had been carefully cultivated over the years. He could still feel their eyes watching him, begging him not to go, but the looming threat of danger was too great to ignore. If they stayed, their lives would be constantly at risk. For the sake of his family's safety, Eddie could not afford to take that perilous gamble.

The salty sea air welcomed them as they arrived in their new home - a quaint yet vibrant city bustling with life and opportunities.

Alison, understanding and supportive as always, believed Eddie when he said their family was in danger. Their daughter Mia was only 3 years old, making it easier to adjust than if she were older and entrenched in her routines. Plus, Alison had heard great things about Adelaide - a beautiful city with plenty of opportunities - so she was happy to relocate for the safety and well-being of her family. It was a bittersweet feeling for Eddie, knowing they had escaped danger but also leaving behind a part of their past lives.

EIGHT

T he ominous storm clouds gathered in the darkening sky above Nick as he stood on the balcony of his penthouse, perched on the 29th floor. The wind howled and roared around him, mirroring his own anger and frustration. He clutched at the railing, knuckles turning white as he gazed out into the city below.

"Damn it!" he shouted, his voice lost in the fierce gusts of wind. "Where is Eddie Sampson?" The trees below bent and swayed under the force of the storm, their leaves rustling with a menacing sound. Lightning flickered in the distance, illuminating the skyline in an eerie glow. The air was charged with electricity, adding to the tension that crackled through Nick's body.

Natas could feel the fury radiating from him. With a soothing tone that seemed to come from everywhere and nowhere at once, he whispered into Nick's mind, "Patience, my friend. We will find him."

Nick's brow furrowed as Natas's words echoed in his thoughts. He had no idea that Eddie, sensing the danger he was in now that his two best friends were either dead or facing lengthy prison sentences, had packed up his wife and child and fled to Australia. The thought of Eddie escaping his grasp fuelled Nick's rage.

"Patience isn't going to bring him back," Nick muttered under his breath. As much as he wanted to make Eddie pay, he knew Natas was right. There were more pressing matters at hand.

He remained on the balcony for a while, allowing his anger to simmer down. He didn't want Shelley to witness him in such a state of fury. He never wanted her to fear him. Once he felt more composed, he re- entered the door and returned to Shelley and their son Dabria now two years old, who were waiting for him in the warmth.

Shelley remained blissfully unaware of the darkness that lurked within him – the presence of Natas and the sinister plans that extended far beyond a simple journey across the world; plans that involved taking over old, abandoned churches and filling them with carefully selected demons. Some were already operating while others were still being prepared.

For Shelley, their upcoming travels were simply an opportunity for adventure and discovery. She could already picture herself strolling through the streets of London, sipping espresso in Italy, admiring Gaudi's architecture in Spain, and indulging in French cuisine. Her eyes sparkled with excitement at the thought of immersing themselves in different cultures and raising their son as a citizen of the world.

"Six to twelve months in each place," Natas instructed Nick as they prepared to embark on their dark pilgrimage. "The people need me. Their desires can only come true with my touch."

Nick nodded, knowing full well the extent of Natas' power. He was fluent in every language, able to charm and manipulate anyone who crossed his path, and his true followers knew they only had to touch him for their own desires to come to fruition.

With Natas coursing through his veins, Nick felt the surge of power within him. He understood that their task of collecting souls was crucial in paving the way for Satan's future dominion as the Dark Lord of the arth. Though they had amassed a significant number thus far, they knew it would still be many years before their goal could be achieved. And so, they diligently worked to build and oversee countless churches, knowing that each one brought them closer to their ultimate destination. Now it was time to visit each of the already established churches.

***

The black SUV pulled up to the Glitz London, its sleek exterior glistening with raindrops. Calvin, ever the loyal servant, held an umbrella aloft as he ushered Nick, Shelley, and Dabria out of the vehicle and into the opulent hotel lobby.

The staff, having been notified of the arrival of their esteemed guests, quickly rushed to greet Lord Nick and his family with a mix of dark and pastel auras.

The manager's aura, a foreboding shade of dark grey, seemed to radiate off of him as he greeted Lord Nick at the entrance of the London Glitz. He eagerly extended his hand for a shake, barely able to contain his excitement at welcoming such a powerful and prestigious visitor. His eyes sparkled with anticipation, and his smile was wide and genuine, showing just how honoured he felt to have

Lord Nick in his establishment. The grand foyer of the Glitz exuded opulence and sophistication, from the crystal chandeliers hanging above to the ornate marble floors below.

"Thank you," Nick replied, his measured tone causing the manager to shiver involuntarily. There was something about the way he spoke that sent a chill down one's spine.

The manager's voice was laced with excitement as he spoke, barely able to contain his eagerness. With a subtle gesture, he directed their attention towards the ornate elevator that awaited them. "Your suite is ready, sir," he announced. He nodded politely at Shelley, who held her young son Dabria close to her chest in a protective embrace.

Following the manager's swift lead, they made their way towards the elevator. The doors, adorned with lavish gold accents, slid open as if at their beck and call. The manager waited until they were all inside before scurrying back to the front desk to bark orders at the already stressed staff – a line of his top employees stood anxiously in the suite, ready to cater to Lord Nick and his entourage's every whim. Shelley marvelled at the extravagance of their surroundings; from the intricate crystal chandelier suspended above to the finely crafted furnishings adorning every inch of the room, it was like stepping into a palace fit for royalty. Compared to the Glitz Hotel in New York, the Glitz here was just as grand, if not even more so. She chided herself for taking it for granted; perhaps she had simply become accustomed to luxurious accommodations.

"Everything seems to be in order," Nick said, his eyes scanning the elegant furnishings and sweeping city views.

"Good," Calvin replied, knowing the importance of pleasing his lord. He had chosen the suite himself, taking great care to ensure that every detail met Nick's exacting standards.

Later that evening, after Dabria had been put to bed, Shelley sat on the plush sofa in the luxurious suite in her silk pyjamas, her laptop open before her. Determined to reclaim her sense of self, she delved into extensive research on how to practice law in London. It had been three long years since the tragedy that claimed the lives of her coworkers and left her without a career. But now, she felt ready to return to work and fight for justice once again. All she had to do was convince Nick that she could still be a devoted mother to their son and a loving wife while balancing the demands of her profession as a lawyer. The thought of stepping back into the world of law filled her with both excitement and nervousness, like standing on the edge of a cliff before taking a leap into the unknown. But she knew it was time to take back control of her life and pursue her passion for seeking justice.

The dim light of the moon cast a soft glow over the room as she called out to her husband, careful not to wake their slumbering child. She was excited now as she believed she held the key to her future - on her laptop, she had found a stack of information on how to practice law in this new place they now called home. According to the documents, she would have to pass a series of rigorous exams and then apply for a license. She turned to Nick, waiting for his opinion with a bated breath, her heart racing with anticipation and nervousness.

He sat down next to her on the couch, his tall and muscular body overshadowing hers as he leaned in close to look at the screen. His violet eyes scanned the information rapidly, despite his wife's success as a lawyer in New York, he felt uneasy about her working. He worried that it would upset her if he brought it up so, he remained silent, trying not to let his inner turmoil show on his face.

She gave him a questioning look and finally, he responded. "Shelley," he started, his voice calm and controlled. "If this is something you truly desire, I will support you. However, I must remind you of the greater purpose we are working towards. Our focus must remain on that goal."

She lifted her gaze to meet his, her crystal blue eyes blazing with unwavering determination. "I understand your concerns, Nick. But this is important to me - I didn't pour my heart and soul into becoming a lawyer just to be a stay-at-home mother and housewife." The dark clouds had gathered outside, casting a sombre grey hue over the city as night fell. The looming threat of rain mirrored the tension in the room.

"Very well," Nick conceded, his voice betraying a hint of reluctance. "I trust your judgment, my love. But remember, my work must never be compromised."

"Thank you, I know," she whispered, leaning into him for comfort.

Nick's arms enveloped Shelley, pulling her close to him. In that moment, his heart was torn between conflicting desires - to see her happy but also to stop her from working for their enemy. For the first time, Natas' voice chimed in, expressing his displeasure at Shelley's career choice and urging Nick to make it clear she could not work as a lawyer. The internal conversation between Nick and Natas grew heated, causing tension to coil through Nick's body. Nick quietly told Natas he would keep Shelley under control, and she would find it impossible to find the time to work, much less study. With that, Natas quietened.

As the night deepened and the quiet of sleep settled over them, Natas stirred restlessly- still brooding over Shelley's desire to work as a lawyer, Nick slumbered peacefully, completely unaware of what was happening

to his body. With a surge of power, Natas seized full control and pulled Shelley towards him roughly. She cried out in shock and fear as he forced himself upon her with brutal force. In a desperate attempt to escape, she thrashed against him and tried to scream, but Natas, fuelled by anger, covered her mouth with his hand to silence her. Nick's consciousness began to surface through the fog of sleep, horrified by the terrible violation being committed by Natas upon his beloved wife. He fought with all his might to regain control and stop the atrocity taking place.

After what felt like an eternity but was just a few minutes, Natas begrudgingly pulled back, allowing Nick to finally regain control. Shelley stumbled off the bed in shock and fled from him, locking herself in the small bathroom. The sound of her shaky breaths echoed off the walls as Nick stood, mortified at what had just occurred. He pleaded for Shelley to come out, and eventually, after much coaxing and reassurance, she emerged with tear-stained cheeks. In a flustered state, Nick attempted to rationalize his actions by claiming he must have been sleepwalking or "sleep raping." Surprisingly, Shelley believed him and tried to diffuse the situation with a nervous laugh. She jokingly suggested that he must have been possessed.

After Nick promised it would never occur again, they both made a pact, not to mention the incident ever again.

Nick's anger flared within him, threatening to boil over as he argued internally with Natas. He warned Natas to leave Shelley alone or risk losing all the work they had done together. Deep down, he knew he couldn't truly control what Natas wanted, but that didn't stop his fury from rising. Despite this, Natas seemed unfazed by

Nick's threat, almost finding it amusing. But in a show of faith, he assured Nick that he would back off from Shelley anyway.

As the weeks went by, Lord Nick continued his work with fervour. The churches flourished under his watchful eye, and their renovations were completed with impeccable taste and precision. His sermons drew larger crowds each day, their congregation swelling in numbers as people flocked to him, seeking solace and material gains. And Lord Nick delivered - with a mere touch of his skin, the power within him surged and wishes were granted, and dreams were fulfilled.

Shelley seemed to have forgotten all about the sleep rape and was happily consumed with the elaborate preparations for her extravagant parties, unable to find time to pursue her dream of returning to work. Each new church opening was marked by a grand celebration orchestrated by Shelley herself. The first party in London was an immense success, drawing in guests from all walks of life. Royalty graced the event, including Prince Anson and his wife, the elegant Duchess Sally. Politicians Tony Flair, John Dresscott, and Gordon Downe made appearances, rubbing elbows with famous sports stars like David Buccham and his stunning wife, Verity. It seemed that word had quickly spread about the Church of Ancient Souls and its healing powers, as well as the whispered rumours of material wealth promised within its walls. Not only did celebrities with darkened souls flock to the party, but also rising stars and hopefuls eager to trade their souls for fame. The air buzzed with excitement and anticipation as guests arrived at the lavish venue, ready to indulge in a night of opulence and intrigue.

Shelley embraced the chance to organize extravagant gatherings, putting aside her desire to go back to work as a lawyer. Her husband couldn't be happier about her choice, though he kept it hidden.

With her son Dabria in tow, Shelley's days were filled with endless wandering through the bustling streets of London. Every corner turned offered new delights for the senses - striking architecture, vibrant street art, and a pulsing energy that seemed to permeate every nook and cranny. The centuries of history that oozed from every brick and cobblestone, combined with the modern flair of a diverse culture, created a unique atmosphere that was impossible to resist. For Shelley, it was a source of pride to watch her son absorb it all, knowing he was experiencing something truly special and unforgettable.

Satan sat upon his imposing throne, his piercing black eyes glinting with malicious satisfaction as he peered into the vision pool before him. The reflections showed his clone, known as Natas, carrying out his orders flawlessly- collecting souls and constructing churches to spread Satan's influence among the mortal realm. Each new soul claimed and church built brought him one step closer to achieving his ultimate goal: complete control over the masses.

But it wasn't just the London branch of Natas' church that flourished under his command. News of miraculous healings and promises of material wealth within its walls had spread like wildfire, fuelled by the efforts of other demons entrusted by Natas to prepare new churches around the world.

His master plan- to establish an army on earth, as well as in hell, was coming to fruition smoothly and he felt a surge of triumphant glee as he watched it unfold in the vision pool before him.

Amid the frenzied bustle of London society, Lord Nick's search for Eddie Sampson was pushed to the far corners of his mind. The hunt had become secondary to his other duties, as Natas could not afford to let it consume him. But even with all the distractions, twelve months flew by in a blur, and Eddie remained out of reach. Nick's thoughts would occasionally drift towards him, like an elusive memory that he couldn't quite grasp, but with each passing day, it became less and less frequent. The city streets were alive with energy, bustling with activity and noise that drowned out any lingering thoughts of the missing man.

NINE

The past ten years had become a blur of cultures and languages, a mosaic of experiences for Shelley and Dabria—a tapestry woven from transient homes. They lived in London, Paris, Rome, Oslo, and Dublin, to name a few.

True to their word, they traversed from country to country, never lingering for more than twelve months in each. Grand openings were orchestrated for every new church they established, with opulent parties of grandeur held in luxurious hotels around the world. Lord Nick was a beloved and well-known figure among the congregations, but it was his wife, Shelley, who stole the hearts of all she met. And Dabria, their son, was celebrated in every country they visited as he grew into a remarkable young man.

Now, in the final of the European countries, as the chill of the northern wind whispered through the trees, Natas' gaze was distant, his thoughts anchored in the past.

In truth, Scotland's call was a siren song he could not ignore. Six more months—what did they matter? Yet to Shelley, they were a promise of settling down, of nurturing the future for Dabria. Dundee awaited the birthplace of Natas' existence—a creation wrought from the darkest of arts. He could feel Natas' pull to that place, an inexorable tug at his soul, or whatever it was.

"New York will be good for us- it's home," Shelley had said with that gentle resolve he'd come to find both comforting and irrevocable. Her words were laced with the unspoken understanding that their son, Dabria, needed stability and roots that could delve deep into the fertile ground of adolescence and education. She had painted a picture of homecoming, a return to normalcy, and Nick had nodded, his assent half-hearted.

"Scotland has its charms," Nick had murmured, his voice the embodiment of restraint, a careful modulation that betrayed nothing of the tempest within. "Six more months, and then New York."

As they settled into the rugged beauty of Scottish moors, Shelley busied herself with plans for Dabria's schooling.

All that remained of the lab when he stumbled upon it was a pile of burnt debris, abandoned and left to decay. Fury coiled within him like a serpent, its venom seeping into his veins. Natas raged at the betrayal, at the lost opportunity to peer into the origins of his cursed life.

"Everything is ash," he muttered to himself, his muscular frame casting a long shadow over the blackened ruins. His eyes flashed red as he surveyed the desolation around him. The scientists, those architects of his life, had fled, leaving only destruction in their wake. the entire science centre was gone- like it had never even existed.

Shelley's warmth seemed a world away as he inscribed the names of the scientists onto his mental list- Dr Penelope MacDonald, Professor Finley Menzies, and Professor Eligh Brown- each now bore a mark of vengeance to be claimed. Nick eagerly savoured the thought of Natas' list; his mind lingered on the satisfaction of completing the final item on his own mental checklist.

The darkness of the Scottish night closed in, a fitting cloak for the rage that festered in his heart. For now, he would wear the mask of the dutiful husband, the attentive father, but beneath it, Natas harboured a growing desire for reprisal against those who dared to play God with the devil's own spawn.

Natas sent out word to all the soul seekers, determined to find Penelope, Finley, and Eligh, who seemed to have vanished without a trace, just like Eddie.

But this time, the messages came back swiftly, and the locations of two of the targets were revealed. Natas wasted no time in devising a plan to reach them, his mind racing with possibilities and contingencies. With the assistance of Calvin, they took flight to their first destination—Eligh's location. The journey was a relatively short and smooth two-and-a-half-hour flight, allowing them to make the trip there and back in one day.

They landed in Marseille; Natas could feel the weight of smug anticipation settle upon him. They had discovered that Eligh resided in a quaint cottage on the outskirts of town, living a solitary life surrounded by fields of vibrant wildflowers.

Pulling up in a sleek, dark grey SUV that hummed almost imperceptibly, Natas and Calvin approached Eligh's cottage on a quiet Saturday morning. The peacefulness of the surrounding countryside seemed to seep into their bones as they walked towards their target. Eligh, lost in thought and unaware of their presence, did not hear the car or their footsteps approaching.

Calvin sat in the car, tapping his fingers on the steering wheel as he waited for Natas to return. Natas approached the quaint cottage

quietly, and saw Eligh on the front veranda; he was putting a chain back on his pushbike; his attention was focused on the task at hand until he heard a sudden noise behind him. Startled, he turned around to find Lord Nick standing there with a sly grin on his face. Nick introduced himself as 'Lord Nick.' "I'm kind of busy, Lord Nick' said Eligh, trying to brush him off. He recognized the name from the new Church that everyone was talking about, claiming he had no interest in religion. He turned back to fixing his bike.

"Oh, perhaps you would know me better as Natas," he continued,

Eligh's face went ashen as the man's words registered in his mind, and he dropped the bike, suddenly realizing that this encounter held more weight than he initially thought.

Before he could even process what was happening, Natas grabbed Eligh by the neck and lifted him off the ground as if he weighed nothing. Panic flooded through him as he struggled against the iron grip, but it was no use.

With a sneer, Natas dragged him into the small cottage, his feet kicking weakly as he tried to scream for help.

"I was deeply disappointed to discover that the science centre has been destroyed," Natas spoke calmly, his voice dripping with malice. Eligh's glasses clattered to the floor as Natas snapped his neck with a sickening crack. The young man's limp body collapsed onto the settee; his eyes stared lifelessly at the ceiling.

With the task accomplished, Natas climbed back into the car and motioned for Calvin to drive. They made their way back to the airport, heading towards Dundee, where Shelley and Dabria were waiting.

Natas instructed Calvin to book his flights for Birmingham the next day as Shelley was eager to return to New York by week's end. The job with Finley needed to be completed quickly. Though Calvin offered to take on the task, Natas insisted on handling it himself, a wicked smirk spreading across his face.

As they returned to their temporary home in Dundee, the elegant

Blyswood Hotel, he found Shelley watching Dabria as he swam with a group of boys in the heated pool. Nick gestured for Shelley to follow him back to their room. As always, after a successful kill, Nick's desire for his wife burned fiercely within him. Dabria remained blissfully unaware of their departure, and Calvin stayed behind to keep an eye on him. Nick whisked Shelley up to their room with an urgent passion, quickly undressing her and making love to her with a fierce hunger.

After a quick change of clothes, they reconvened with Dabria in the elegant dining room. His excitement was palpable as he eagerly discussed their upcoming trip to New York - a city he hadn't visited since he was a toddler. Despite not having any real memories of the place, Shelley's enchanting stories made him feel like it was home. He bombarded his father, Lord Nick, with questions about their itinerary - wanting to know every detail and if they could leave tomorrow. Nick smiled at his son's enthusiasm, but there was still a pressing business matter that needed his attention. He regretted not flying directly from Marseille to Birmingham now, but he reminded Dabria to be patient.

They had plenty of time, and New York would still be waiting for them at the end of the week, just as magnificent and bustling as ever.

They took the earliest flight to Birmingham and landed a little after 7 am. The roads were quiet on a Sunday morning, and the sun was just beginning to rise over the sleepy city. By 7:30, they had parked outside Finley's flat on Water Street, the birds chirping their morning songs in the background. Natas sat with Calvin in the car, watching and waiting for any signs of life from inside the flat. Half an hour later, an old man emerged, dressed in his Sunday best. He was on his way to church, wearing a tweed sports coat and gloves to keep out the cold, along with a chocolate brown scarf draped around his neck. Finley approached him from down the path, but before he could reach him, Natas stepped out and blocked his path. "You don't seem to recognize me, Professor," Natas said with a sly smile.

Finley's thick Scottish accent came through as he replied, "Oh, I do apologize. I am quite busy at the moment. Perhaps you can come back after church."

Natas let out a deep, demonic laugh that caused Finley to shudder. He tried to step around Natas, but he was having none of it. "Let's walk together, Professor Menzies," Natas offered as he fell into step beside Finley.

As they turned off the path and onto a footpath, Finley couldn't help but feel nervous. He tried to maintain a pleasant demeanour towards his visitor as he asked," How can I help you, Mr...Mr?"

"My name is Lord Nick," Natas replied with a hint of pride. "Maybe you have heard of me? I am the Lord of the Church of Ancient Souls."

Finley hesitated before responding," Oh yes, I have heard of you. But I'm afraid that is not MY church, Lord Nick. I am not heading there, and I will not be persuaded."

Natas remained silent for a while as they walked alongside each other. As they passed through a nearby park, Natas suddenly spoke up again. "Perhaps you have heard of my 'other name'?" he asked with a sly grin, his voice dripping with malice. "Natas?"

Finley stumbled at the mention of the name, fear etched across his face. He remembered back to the cloning of Satan and Satan announcing that he would call him Natas - a name that still brought nightmares after all these years.

They were now stopped in the middle of the park, not another person in sight. "I was very disappointed when I found out your lab had burned to the ground," Natas told him, his tone cold and calculating.

Before Finley could react, Natas lunged forward and grabbed him by the neck, twisting it until he heard the sickening sound of bones breaking. Finley died instantly, his lifeless body slumped over on a nearby bench, his eyes staring vacantly ahead.

Natas brushed off his coat and turned back towards Calvin in the waiting car. With a simple nod, he signalled for Calvin to drive away, leaving behind the lifeless body of Professor Menzies and any trace of their encounter on the quiet Sunday morning.

***

After years of constant travel and adventure, they finally settled back in the United States. Their new home, a lavish sanctuary nestled in Central Park South, was a testament to their elevated status in society. Dabria, who had always been bright and curious, continued to excel in school, his intellect shining like a beacon in their opulent surroundings.

After his return to the United States, Nick's mind was consumed by thoughts of finding Eddie Sampson. Despite his demons' best efforts in helping with the task, every night as he laid on his opulent bedding with its shimmering diamond patterns and intricate silk embroidery, his thoughts were consumed with questions of Eddie's whereabouts and the likelihood of ever tracking him down. The weight of this obsession hung heavy in the air, overshadowing even the luxurious surroundings of his bedroom. Now Penelope Mac Donald was also missing.

TEN

Mia Simpson waited perched with precision on the rough stone fence that marked the boundary of her Brighton home. The early morning sun warmed her school uniform, but a chill still ran through her as she felt the jagged edges of the stones against her bare legs. She glanced down at her phone, resisting the temptation to check her social media, knowing that her friend Laura would arrive any moment.

From her perch, she had a perfect view of the beach, its sparkling waters lapping gently against the shore. As she turned her head to look back down the street, she spotted Laura rounding the corner and waving energetically. Mia returned the gesture and pushed herself off the fence, slinging her heavy backpack over one shoulder as she walked towards her friend.

For the past four and a half years, they had started their day walking to high school side by side. They had formed a strong bond since their first encounter on the playground in primary school and had been inseparable ever since.

They were almost complete opposites in appearance—Mia, with her sun-kissed blonde hair and piercing blue eyes, tall and lean; while Laura, with dark eyes and straight black hair, was a bit shorter in height but with a curvier figure that made her mistakenly appear chunky.

Despite their outward differences, they shared many similarities. Both were diligent students, pouring over textbooks and earning top grades in their classes. They had grand plans for university after high school - both were fascinated by the field of Law, though uncertain about whether they wanted to pursue a career as lawyers or cops. Unlike the majority of their classmates who revelled in partying and socializing, these two stuck to themselves and didn't have any close friends besides each other.

Although they were both attractive young ladies, their reserved and introverted natures often labelled them "nerdy" among their classmates.

As their feet fell in sync beside each other, it was evident that their friendship surpassed any surface-level differences. Chattering excitedly, they eagerly discussed their upcoming plans for the formal which was only six weeks away. They had made a pact at the beginning of the year to go together, not wanting to wait and hope for someone to ask them out. And if by chance one of them was asked and the other wasn't, they had promised to decline and stick to their original plan of attending together. They excitedly talked about their plans to go shopping on the weekend, their energy radiating through the otherwise quiet suburban neighbourhood as they made their way toward school.

On the edge of the oval, where they always met for lunch, Mia sat on the soft green grass with her lunchbox in her lap. She watched as a group of younger boys ran around, kicking a football back and forth. In other areas of the grounds, groups had started to gather, chatting and laughing.

As she leisurely surveyed her surroundings, absently nibbling on her sandwich, her eyes landed on the figure of Mark Mahoney. He was like a vision to her, with chiselled features and a dazzling smile. She caught herself gazing at him intently until she realized he was walking towards her, his strides purposeful and confident- he was one of the popular boys at Brighton High School. He was a footy jock, with good looks and a certain charm that drew people to him. As he approached, Mia felt a sudden rush of anxiety wash over her, knowing he was coming straight towards her.

Mark crouched down beside her, flashing a charming smile. "Hello, Mia," he greeted. "It's not like you to be alone. Where's your shadow?" He was trying to be funny.

Mia couldn't help but smile back. "You mean Laura? She'll be here soon."

She tried to keep her tone casual, but her voice came out high-pitched and squeaky.

"Well, I'm glad I caught you alone," Mark continued, causing her to blush "I've been wanting to ask - would you come to the formal with me?"

Feeling flustered, Mia stumbled over her words. What she wanted to say was that she had already promised to go with Laura, but what came out instead was: "Umm, can I say maybe?" Her blush deepened and Mark's grin widened.

He seemed to understand her hesitation and added, "Laura has a date with Connor—at least she does if she says yes." His grin only grew wider as Mia's shocked expression confirmed it all. Standing up from his crouched position, Mark said, "Let me know on Monday. You and Laura can work out what you both want to do over the weekend." With a nod from Mia, Mark turned and made his way back towards the school building.

Mia sat there holding her sandwich, wondering if she was that easy to read. Why would someone popular like Mark want to take her to the formal? And it was a strange coincidence how they had just discussed the formal with Laura this morning, and now Mark Mahoney was asking her out- it all seemed so bizarre to her. Before she could dwell on it too long, Laura came rushing around the corner and made a beeline for her.

"Oh my gosh!" she exclaimed as she plopped herself down on the grass beside Mia. "Connor Davies just asked me to be his date at the formal! Can you believe it? Mr. Popular!"

Mia chuckled, and Laura went on: "Well, of course I'll tell him no if you want. I mean, if you don't have a date. That's the deal, right?"

Laura rambled on excitedly while Mia lay back on the grass, taking in the blue sky above. "Funny enough," she said with a grin, "Mark Mahoney asked me to the formal too."

Laura's eyes widened in surprise. "No way! What did you say?"

"I said I'll let him know on Monday," Mia replied with a shrug.

The girls giggled, lounging in the soft grass and soaking up the sun's warmth. It was hard to believe that after four and a half years of high school, the popular guys were suddenly taking notice of them. "It's insane how they never paid attention to us before," Mia marvelled.

"Well, they probably ran out of other options," Laura chimed in with a hint of sarcasm. The girls continued to chatter, discussing their plans for Saturday's shopping trip to find new dresses for the upcoming event. Avoiding the obvious topic of whether or not they would accept dates from Mark and Conner, they both agreed to take some time to think it over before making any decisions. As they soaked up the warmth and beauty of the day, they knew that their discussion could wait until Saturday.

Mark Mahoney was only 17 years old, yet his soul was pitch black. His parents had taken him to a new Church when they were on holiday in New York four years ago. The Mahoneys were staying with friends in the bustling city, and their hosts had introduced them to a new religion. They spoke of miraculous healings - everything from physical disabilities to behavioral problems - all attributed to their Lord's intervention. The stories were compelling, and Mark's parents were eager for their son to experience this form of salvation. Although there was nothing serious wrong with Mark, he showed signs of rebellion even at a young age. His parents feared he would end up on the wrong side of the law if left unchecked. And so, they brought him to be "healed" or "saved," as some liked to call it.

After that fateful day, Mark transformed into an exemplary student - excelling in all areas with a laser focus and determination. His father's dreams of athletic glory were realized as Mark dominated the field, while his mother's wishes for academic success were met with straight As and commendations from teachers. Yet, despite his outward achievements, there was an unsettling darkness about him. His once bright eyes now seemed dull and devoid of emotion. A cruel side to him had emerged, causing animals to shrink away and leaving a trail of shattered hearts behind with the girls he dated. They could have shared stories of his coldness and cruelty, but they feared losing their social standing among the popular football crowd. For they could sense the darkness within him and feared what he may be capable of if provoked. Little did they know, Mark was also eagerly awaiting the call to fulfill his lord's bidding - eager to unleash that darkness upon the world.

In this vast land of Australia, there were fewer darkened souls compared to other countries where the Church of Ancient Souls had been implemented. For 17 years, its presence had not yet touched these soils, but its influence could still be felt from afar.

Mark, like all other darkened souls, was well aware of Lord Nick's relentless pursuit of the elusive Sampson family - Eddie, Alison, and their daughter Mia. From the moment he heard her unmistakable American twang, he had a gut feeling about Mia. At first, he couldn't quite pinpoint why, but as time passed by, he began to connect the dots and realized that Mia Simpson was most likely Mia Sampson. He had spoken to some of the other local kids who knew her, but none seemed to have any substantial knowledge about her - she was a quiet, unassuming girl with a nerdy disposition. But Mark was determined to unravel the truth.

His research led him to discover that Mia's mother was indeed named Alison, and her father was a lawyer, but none of the other students could remember his name since he had never visited the school. With near certainty, he believed he had uncovered the identity of the mysterious family sought after by Lord Nick. Anticipation coursed through his veins as he sent word and eagerly awaited word from his master via the demon shadows.

If his hunch proved correct, Mark was sure to be commended for this valuable find and possibly even rewarded with his own church in Brighton. So he kept a watchful eye on Mia, biding his time until Lord Nick arrived in this corner of the world.

With his entire entourage in tow - including maids and goons - Nicholas Green eagerly relocated his family to the serene beachside suburb of Brighton in Adelaide, South Australia. For years, he had been considering expanding his work and establishing new churches for his devoted followers in Australia. And now, with the news from Mark Mahoney, his long-awaited opportunity for revenge against Eddie Sampson had finally arrived. It seemed almost too good to be true - after all these years, he had never truly given up hope of finding Eddie and his family, but there were moments where he doubted if they even still existed, having vanished without a trace. But now, Nicholas felt a sense of satisfaction knowing that he was one step closer to fulfilling his ultimate goal.

Shelley and Dabria were filled with anticipation as they embarked on their next adventure. Years of traveling to open new churches and spread the word of The Church Of Ancient Souls had instilled in them a sense of wanderlust, and they eagerly embraced the idea of exploring new lands.

Brighton, a charming suburb of Adelaide, also known as the city of Churches, was a sight to behold. Ironically, it was about to welcome a whole new kind of church into its midst. The summer sun glistened on the white sandy beaches while hip cafes buzzed with energy.

Little did they know, Nick had his own ulterior motive for abruptly moving them to this idyllic location.

Their new home on the esplanade was a sight to behold. The grand, three-story mansion stood tall and proud, overlooking the glistening waters of Brighton Beach. Dabria's father had insisted he attend Brighton High School, scoffing at the idea of sending him to a Catholic school. As a senior in New York, Dabria was a year younger than his classmates at Brighton but quickly found his place among them. The other students were curious and eager to hear about his travels around the world. As the last term began, Dabria knew that exams were looming, but all anyone could talk about was the upcoming formal dance.

A number of invitations flooded in from girls who wanted Dabria as their date. However, he politely declined each offer, determined to focus on his impending exams. He wasn't sure if he even wanted to attend the event at all, but the possibility lingered in the back of his mind, tempting him with promises of excitement and adventure. But for now, he remained dedicated to his studies.

Even the guys were drawn to him, eagerly seeking his friendship. One particular guy, Mark Mahoney, seemed almost obsessed with befriending him, constantly hovering around and trying to strike up a conversation. Dabria couldn't shake off a strange feeling about him and made a conscious effort to avoid his company. It was as if there was an invisible force between them, pushing him away from his strange aura.

One Saturday morning, just a few weeks after moving, while out for his usual beachside run, Dabria stumbled upon Mia and Laura launching their standup paddleboards. Intrigued by the unique water sport he had never tried before, he stopped to chat with them. They kindly offered to teach him how to paddleboard, and before he knew it, they were effortlessly gliding through the waves together. Despite his experience with surfing and other water sports, such as water skiing and kayaking, he had never felt the serene rush of stand-up paddleboarding. With Mia and Laura as his guides, he fully immersed himself in this new activity for the entire morning, forming a strong bond of friendship along the way.

As the days passed, Dabria, Mia, and Laura grew closer, their friendship solidifying with each passing conversation. The routine of walking to school together quickly became a tradition for Dabria, Mia, and Laura. They would meet at Mia's front fence every morning, their laughter and chatter filling the quiet streets.

While they waited for Laura one morning, Dabria inquired about Mia's accent. She joked that it was due to her parents' influence and clarified that she was actually a full-fledged Aussie, specifically an 'Adelaidian' as she liked to call herself since she had lived there since she was just three years old. Dabria with his much more pronounced American accent thought she was hilarious and told her he couldn't wait until he also could be classed as an Adelaidian.

Despite living just meters from each other, their parents were unaware of the trio's newfound friendship. Mia revelled in the refreshing change of routine. At home, loneliness and monotony were all too familiar, with her parents consumed by work and rarely present. Her mother, especially, was rarely at home due to her new passion for yoga. With her job and yoga taking up most of her time, she wasn't around much. She was constantly raving about how rejuvenated she felt now that she was practicing yoga under the guidance of her instructor, Penny Donald. Despite her mother's attempts to involve her, Mia refused to join in on the yoga craze. Alison and Penny's bond extended far beyond their yoga sessions, weaving its way into every aspect of their lives. They would often rendezvous for a leisurely lunch or a steaming cup of coffee, eagerly exchanging stories and updates on their lives.

With Dabria and Laura by her side, Mia felt alive and happier than she could remember.

As the three of them strolled down the tree-lined street towards school, Dabria couldn't help but notice how Mia seemed to glow in the morning sunlight. Her long blonde locks cascaded over her shoulders, reflecting golden hues and framing her face in a halo of light. Her bright blue eyes shone like sapphires as she chattered excitedly about their plans for the day.

Strangely enough, it seemed as though Dabria was seeing Mia for the first time. He couldn't believe he had never noticed how her hair danced in the gentle breeze or how her eyes lit up when she talked about something she loved. It was almost as if she had transformed into a radiant being overnight.

Unbeknownst to Dabria, Mia had also been secretly admiring him for some time now. She was captivated by his sharp intellect and well-travelled stories, often asking him questions about different countries and cultures he had experienced. They bonded over their mutual love for adventure sports, and their conversations were always filled with lively discussions about new activities they wanted to try together. Their friendship continued to grow stronger each day at school as well. They sat next to each other in classes whenever possible and studied together during free time.

But amidst all the fun times they shared, there was an underlying tension that neither of them could quite understand. Whenever they were alone together, there was an unspoken chemistry between them that made both of them feel giddy yet nervous at the same time.

As weeks went by, Laura felt a little left out. She had noticed the growing closeness between Dabria and Mia, and it made her feel uneasy. While she was happy for her friends to have formed such a strong bond, she couldn't shake off the feeling that she was being left behind.

It all came to a head one afternoon when Dabria and Mia were planning their next adventure together. They were excitedly discussing going rock climbing at a nearby mountain when Laura suddenly interrupted them.

"Can I come too?" she blurted out, feeling guilty for not being as close to Dabria as Mia was.

Dabria and Mia exchanged a look before turning to Laura with slightly hesitant expressions.

"I mean, if you want," Mia said uncertainly. "But it's kind of an intense climb."

Laura's heart sank. She could tell they didn't really want her to come along. Feeling hurt and rejected, she mumbled something about having other plans and quickly walked away.

That night, as she lay in bed replaying the scene in her head, Laura felt angry at herself for feeling jealous of her friends' friendship. But at the same time, she couldn't shake off the nagging feeling that she was losing her two closest friends.

One Saturday morning, there was a knock on the door, and Eddie answered it to find a young man standing on their porch. He introduced himself as Dabria Green and asked if Mia was home. After shaking his hand and inviting him in, Eddie called out for Mia. He looked at Dabria carefully, and he couldn't shake off a feeling of familiarity but couldn't quite place it. Mia came out, and the two left to meet Laura at the beach as planned. Along the way, they talked and laughed like old friends, enjoying each other's company without a care in the world. The sun shone down on them as they walked along the beach, creating a picturesque scene of three friends enjoying their weekend together.

Laura was trying her best to relax and enjoy spending time with her friends. She had come to accept that it was a normal part of life for Mia to meet someone and develop feelings for them, even though she hadn't expected it to happen so soon. She wondered if Mia and Dabria were aware of their growing affection for each other since they were still just friends at the moment.

The warm sun beat down on Eddie and Alison as they strolled hand in hand along the sandy foreshore, their stomachs content after a delicious lunch at a cozy seaside cafe.

But as they neared their home, Eddie couldn't shake the strange feeling of being watched. He froze and scanned the surroundings - the beach, the houses overlooking it - Seeing nothing out of the ordinary, he brushed off the sensation but still hurried Alison along.

Upon arriving home, Mia and her friends were lounging on the deck. Dabria quickly jumped up from his seat and eagerly re-introduced himself to Mia's parents, just in case they had forgotten him. Eddie couldn't quite place where he knew Dabria from until it hit him like a ton of bricks - 'Dabria Green'- he was Nicholas and Shelley Green's son. Horrified, he pulled Alison aside in the kitchen to share his discovery.

As the sun began its descent and the shadows grew longer, Dabria and Laura said their goodbyes and left for home. Mia's parents sat her down, their faces etched with concern. They forbade her from ever seeing that boy again, Mia's heart raced with anger, her mind reeling with disbelief at their sudden decision. She suddenly felt like a prisoner in her own home, trapped by their rigid rules and judgmental views. When she pressed for an explanation, all they could offer was vague statements about his family being "bad news." But Mia couldn't understand why they would pass such harsh judgments without even giving him a chance.

As the evening wore on Mia couldn't shake off the feeling of betrayal and injustice. She couldn't imagine never seeing him again.

In the dark stillness of their bedroom, Eddie and Alison whispered urgently to each other. They knew they were in grave danger now that Nicholas Green - or Lord Nick, as he preferred to be called - had found them. They huddled close together as they discussed their limited options for safety. Relocating once again seemed inevitable.

They could already imagine the anger and disappointment on

Mia's face when she found out. She had her whole future planned out, and this sudden move would throw a wrench in all of it. Alison suggested waiting until after the Year 12 formal, knowing how much her daughter was looking forward to it. She had already bought a dress and had a date lined up with a boy named Mark, whom Eddie had never met before. With the dance only a week away, Eddie agreed to postpone their move until after that night. But he made it clear that they would have to pack up and leave immediately afterward.

As they continued to discuss their plans, Alison stroked Eddie's hand reassuringly. Weighing up their options -They decided to move to London, hoping they could start fresh without fear of being tracked down by Nicholas.

Mia looked absolutely stunning in her formal gown, a delicate shade of pale blue that exposed one shoulder completely. Her parents gushed at her as she gracefully walked out onto the deck where they were sitting, enjoying the warm summer breeze and sipping on glasses of wine.

The doorbell suddenly sounded, causing Mia to hold her breath. "I'll get it," she said, turning to head back through the house. But her father stopped her, his strong hand resting on her shoulder.

"I'll get it, Mia. I want to meet this young man before he takes you out." Eddie strode to the front door and swung it open. "You must be Mark," he said, putting his hand out for the young man to shake. "Eddie Simpson."

Mark shook his hand, a smirk playing across his face as he confirmed his suspicions - this was Eddie Sampson, as Lord Nick had mentioned. His mind raced with the idea of somehow getting a message to him. He knew Lord Nick was close by now, but not exactly how close. Eddie ushered him inside and through the house to the deck, where Mia and her mother were waiting.

"Let's go," Mia said almost immediately, eager to get out of the house. But before they could leave, Alison Simpson stepped in front of them and shook Mark's hand, introducing herself before Mia could push past.

"Take good care of our girl," she said with a warm smile.

Rolling her eyes at her parents' overprotective nature, Mia finally managed to step past them and take Mark's hand as they made their way out to his waiting car.

He let go of her hand as she reached the passenger side and told her she looked beautiful before opening the door for her. As Mia climbed into the sleek black Mustang, she couldn't help but be impressed by Mark's choice of vehicle. He explained that it was a gift from his parents for getting good grades, and they set off towards Glenelg with the powerful engine shattering the stillness of the night.

Mia sat in the car, staring out the window as they drove to the dance. She had put on a brave face, covering her tear-stained cheeks with layers of makeup, but her heart still felt heavy and broken. Her parents' decision to forbid her from seeing Dabria weighed heavily on her mind, and she couldn't bring herself to talk about it with Mark.

As they neared the venue, Mia's thoughts turned to Laura. Her best friend would be at the dance, and she hoped it would give her a chance to talk things over with her and find some solace. Laura knew everything that was going on with Dabria and her parents. She told Laura that Dabria knows about her parents' strict rules, and how they had banned her from seeing him, and he seemed just as confused and hurt by their judgment. He got angry and walked away after exclaiming that his family was not 'bad news', with his father being a preacher for 'God's sake'.

But Dabria's absence at school for the rest of the week and Laura's updates that he wasn't responding to any texts or calls except to say he wasn't feeling well only added to Mia's worries. The weight of the situation felt almost suffocating as they pulled up to the dance venue.

Mia and Mark entered the Hotel at Glenelg, aptly named 'The Grand'; Laura stood waiting just inside the double doors. She waved excitedly as she spotted them, her eyes sparkling with anticipation. The entrance was adorned with a luxurious red carpet, a popular spot for photos on school formal night. No doubt these snapshots would end up in the yearbook and available for purchase in the coming weeks. Laura looked breathtaking in her white halter neck dress, its sleek fabric hugging her every curve. The soft glow of the chandeliers above highlighted her perfectly braided chignon and flawlessly applied makeup and nails, all professionally done. As Mia took in her friend's stunning appearance, she felt a twinge of guilt for bailing on their plans to get ready together - she had spent hours crying over Dabria instead. She managed to throw together some decent makeup, but her hair remained its usual wild and untamed self. Laura didn't seem to mind, embracing Mia with a warm hug before they made their way to the bathroom, temporarily excusing themselves from their dates' company.

ELEVEN

Mia and Laura spent the time at the school formal talking about what had happened with Dabria, the events weighing heavily on their minds. Mia's heart ached as she confided in her friend about her feelings for Dabria, feelings that she had barely acknowledged to herself until now. But with the knowledge that she was forbidden from seeing him, the grief and uncertainty consumed her.

Despite the loud music and chatter of the crowded room, they found a quiet corner to sit together. The dim lights cast shadows over the dancing and raucous conversations surrounding them. Mark and Conner didn't seem to mind being ditched; they were seen now and then dancing with other girls on the crowded dance floor. While supposedly an alcohol-free event, both boys seemed suspiciously drunk as they stumbled over to Mia and Laura towards the end of the formal.

Mark eagerly told Mia about a party happening on the 5th floor, insisting that it was where all the fun was. Exhausted and wanting nothing more than to go home, both girls hesitantly declined, and Conner offered to drive Laura home.

Mia hugged her friend goodbye and watched her walk towards the double doors with Conner, but as they reached the doors, Laura told Conner she had ordered an Uber because she didn't want to get into a car with him. After all, he had obviously been drinking. With his plans ruined, Conner turned back to Mia and Mark, determined to salvage his night. He whispered to Mia that Dabria had arrived not too long ago and had been whisked away by some other girls to the party on the 5th floor. Suddenly intrigued, Mia eagerly agreed to go with them to the party.

With Mia sandwiched between the two jocks, Mark and Conner, they made their way towards the elevator. Her heart fluttered with excitement at the thought of seeing Dabria again, but she couldn't shake off her unease at being alone with these two intimidating boys who seemed a little too intrigued by her.

Both boys ogled her as if she were a valuable trophy, making her feel uncomfortable and making her wish she had gone home with Laura.

When the elevator finally opened, she quickly exited before them. However, she overheard Mark question Conner about whether Dabria was really at the party, and she turned to see Conner nodding. Mia couldn't understand why Mark was so interested in Dabria, although she did remember him being unusually friendly towards him at school. Dabria found it peculiar but didn't dwell on it too much. As they walked, the sound of their footsteps echoed through the hallway, and Mia's mind raced with anticipation for what was to come.

The room was a luxurious suite, complete with a separate bedroom, a well-equipped kitchenette, and multiple plush lounges. From the open doorway, Mia's eyes were drawn to the balcony, where Dabria was in the centre of a group of beautiful girls, all dressed to the nines for their school formal with fancy dresses and expertly applied makeup. He held a beer in one hand and leaned against the railing in a casual yet confident stance. Mia's heart fluttered at the sight of him, and she barely registered that she was blocking the doorway until Mark put his hands on her waist and nudged her from behind. Annoyed, she pushed his hands off and made her way inside. She felt out of place as she entered the room; everyone was looking at her, and she was regretting her decision to come. Mia's gaze lingered on Dabria, feeling both drawn to and intimidated by his presence among such beauty. He looked over, and his smile widened, causing the girls around him to turn and see who he was smiling at. As she made her way towards him, Mark suddenly appeared out of nowhere, pushing past with a sense of urgency. He grabbed Dabria's hand and pumped it with a firm grip, exclaiming how good it was to see him there. Dabria politely shook his hand and quickly let go, trying to avoid any further conversation. Mark, however, was still attempting to make small talk, but Dabria's attention was elsewhere as Mia made her way through the room towards them.

Their eyes met, and both of their smiles grew wider, completely oblivious to anyone else around them. It was clear to everyone that these two were only interested in each other. Even Mark got the hint and shuffled off in a different direction, leaving them alone on the balcony. But he watched from just inside with a less-than-happy expression on his face. He weighed his options, wondering what he could do to appease his Lord.

He couldn't figure Dabria out—he was the son of his Lord—yet seemed unaffected by it all. Did he even know who Mia really was? Was he truly working for Lord Nick, or was his interest in Mia genuine? He pondered his questions silently as he observed the couple before him.

As they conversed on the balcony, their words were laden with intensity and longing. Forbidden from seeing each other, their emotions had only grown stronger. Dabria, unable to get a ticket to attend the formal at such a late date, could only hope that Mia would show up for the after-party as well.

The rest of the party was alive and pulsing inside the suite, but these two remained outside on the balcony in their own private world. They talked fervently about their feelings for each other, completely absorbed in one another's company. Eventually, Dabria wrapped his arms around Mia in a tight embrace before offering to get her a drink. As he finished his beer, she requested water, and he chuckled at her unconventional choice. With a promise to do his best to find it, he left her on the balcony alone as he made his way through the bustling crowd to search for their beverages.

Mia turned away from the lively party, her eyes drawn to the breathtaking view of Glenelg beach. Despite the late hour - she guessed it was past midnight - there were still numerous figures moving about on the cobbled stones below. Some appeared to be revellers, their laughter and chatter carrying up to her on the balmy summer breeze, while others strolled leisurely, taking in the warm evening air. The moon cast a shimmering light over the water, causing it to dance and sparkle like a thousand diamonds. Mia felt a sense of peace and contentment wash over her as she gazed out at the tranquil scene before her.

In one swift motion, the doors to the balcony flew open with a loud bang. Mia spun around, startled and confused. She hadn't even noticed Dabria closing the doors as he went inside in search of drinks. But it wasn't Dabria standing there- it was Mark, and he was angry and drunk.

"You little bitch," he slurred, his words slurring together. "You came to the party with me, and now you're getting it on with another guy?" He lunged forward, grabbing her wrists and pushing her back against the balustrade.

Mia felt a surge of fear rise up in her chest as she tried to push him away. "You're hurting me, Mark," she said, trying to keep her voice calm. She glanced past him, searching for any sign of Dabria's return. But no one seemed to be paying attention to them.

His grip tightened on her wrists, his whole weight pressing against her now. He started pulling at her dress, trying to lift it up. "What are you doing?" she demanded through clenched teeth, still struggling against him.

"I'm having you- that's what I'm doing," Mark spat out. With a sudden burst of strength, he flung her around like a rag doll so that her back was now facing him. Mia could feel the fabric of her dress being yanked up, and panic coursed through her veins.

She fought back with all her might, but Mark was bigger and stronger than she was. He lifted her off the ground, still trying to pull her dress up. And then suddenly, she felt herself falling.

For a split second, time seemed to slow down as she hurtled towards the ground, gravity pulling her down faster and faster. She let out a blood-curdling scream as she fell face-first off the balcony.

She didn't hit the ground per se, but rather landed on a man who was out for an evening walk. The impact of her fall flattened him, sending him sprawling onto the pavement. He was an aboriginal Ngangkari, or witch doctor, known as Daku Gaari. He was a revered healer and, therefore, protected by an angel at all times. But at this moment, he had been in the wrong place at the wrong time. Their two bodies collided, killing them both instantly, and their spirits rose into the sky with the angel, becoming entwined. On the ground, a crowd had quickly gathered around the chaotic scene. Among them were a married couple- an off-duty doctor and a nurse. With swift precision and skill, they began performing CPR on the two victims as they waited for an ambulance to arrive. The air was thick with panic and grief as onlookers stood by helplessly watching. The blaring sirens of the ambulance pierced through the thick silence of the bloody scene. The nurse's voice echoed across the chaos, calling out to her Doctor husband in a mixture of relief and urgency. "I've got a pulse!" Mia lay on the ground, her limp body now miraculously revived. Her pale skin contrasted starkly against the dark pool of blood that surrounded her. The smell of antiseptic and fear lingered in the air as the medical team rushed to stabilize her.

Her spirit, now combined with the Ngangkari, had re-entered her body, and the angel, invisible to bystanders, wrapped her gently with its wings. She was unresponsive but still breathing as the paramedics carefully placed her into the ambulance and raced off into the darkness, sirens wailing, heading towards the hospital.

Mia's parents waited anxiously at her bedside, their faces etched with worry and exhaustion from days of constant vigil. They had put their plans to move to London on hold, their sole focus now on their precious daughter who lay unmoving in the hospital bed. The doctors could offer no concrete answers as to why she was taking so long to wake up, only that she was lucky to still be alive. But Eddie and Alison could not see any luck in this situation - their daughter had fallen from a 5th-story balcony at a party she shouldn't have been at. And to make matters worse, it was Dabria Green, the boy she wasn't supposed to be seeing, who had come knocking frantically on their door in the middle of the night to tell them of the accident. Eddie couldn't shake off his suspicion that this was more than just an accident - after all, Dabria's father, the enigmatic Lord Nick, had already killed some of his friends and ruined his other best friend's life. And Eddie knew he was here in Brighton for one reason: to exact revenge on him.

TWELVE

fter eleven weeks of uncertainty, Mia slowly opened her eyes to the harsh, fluorescent lights of the hospital room. The pungent smell of antiseptic filled her nostrils, and the steady beeping of machines invaded her ears.

She slowly lifted her hand and reached out for her mother's cool touch beside her. As she grasped her hand, a gasp escaped her lips, jolting Eddie from his slumber in the chair next to her bed. He frantically called for a nurse or doctor, anyone who could help.

In the quiet of the night, at three am, they heard the soft patter of feet approaching their room. A young nurse appeared, looking weary and worn. Despite her exhaustion, she smiled warmly at Mia.

"You're awake," she said softly to Mia as she approached the bed.

"How are you feeling?" The nurse asked, gently picking up Mia's right wrist and feeling for her pulse, checking the time on her small fob watch attached to her uniform she asked, "Can you tell me your name?"

Mia answered weakly, "Yes, Mia Simpson."

The nurse then began asking Mia questions, trying to determine if she had suffered any brain damage. Her parents held their breaths, waiting for each answer, relief washing over them when the nurse turned to them and said that Mia seemed to be doing well.

She filled in Mia's chart after completing the rest of her observations, informing them that she would let the doctors know when they arrived at 7am. As she left the room, the sound of machines beeping, and distant chatter filled the otherwise silent ward. Mia closed her eyes again, she had no idea how she had ended up here and her brain felt foggy, 'crowded' she thought as she drifted back off to sleep.

When she woke again, the hospital room was a flurry of activity. Doctors and nurses bustled about, moving quickly from patient to patient. In the corner, her parents stood with concerned looks on their faces, talking to a man and a woman with stethoscopes draped around their necks, Mia determined they were most likely her doctors.

Seeing her stir, they smiled warmly at Mia before approaching her bedside. Doctor Kane Allen and Doctor Ashlee Bishop introduced themselves to Mia, her parents stepped back, allowing the doctors to take over. They asked similar questions to the ones she had been asked by the young nurse earlier- but in a much more serious and clinical tone.

After a brief conversation, the doctors informed Mia that she would need to undergo a brain scan to assess any potential damage. Once they obtained the results, they would determine if she was able to walk. One of the doctors signalled for a nurse and asked her to unhook the monitors attached to her body before she was wheeled away by a kind orderly for the scan.

Upon returning to her room, she found a tray of food waiting for her. Despite it being just a simple sandwich and juice, she discovered her appetite had returned with a vengeance. She devoured the meal eagerly, grateful for something substantial in her stomach.

"Well," stated Doctor Allen, "the good news is that your brain appears to be functioning normally. You didn't suffer any major trauma or damage."

Mia let out a sigh of relief.

The following day, the doctors paid another visit to Mia, and this time, they sent her to a physical therapist to evaluate her leg strength. They were astounded that she had survived such a massive fall with only some cracked ribs.

She was physically frail, and walking no longer came as naturally as it once had. But after being unconscious for an extended period of time, this was to be expected, according to the physiotherapist who worked with her. Dr. Bishop summed up, "After our examination, it seems you have a few cracked ribs but no other physical injuries." "We are pleased to discharge you from the hospital to go home into your parent's care.

Just remember to take it easy during your recovery. Your memory of the accident may come back, but in some cases, it doesn't - it's your brain's way of protecting you".

With a gentle hand on Mia's shoulder, Alison insisted, "You should come to yoga with me, Mia. It will be incredibly beneficial for your recovery." Her eyes shone with enthusiasm, and she raved about her incredible instructor, Penny. Without hesitation, she pulled out her phone and dialled Penny's number as they left the hospital. Determined to make it happen, Alison refused to take no for an answer.

Like two vigilant mother hawks, Eddie and Alison hovered over Mia's bedside, as two fierce hawks protect their precious nest. Their watchful eyes never strayed from her side, constantly assessing her every move. Penny came by regularly to provide private yoga lessons, hoping to aid in the young woman's recovery. But despite their efforts, Mia still felt weighed down by the weight of her recent accident. Despite the care and attention surrounding her, she still felt overwhelmed by it all, weighed down by the lack of memory of her fall. She couldn't shake the feeling of a blockage in her mind, as if something was holding her thoughts captive. The details of the accident were a blur; she recalled being on the balcony with Dabria, but everything after that was hazy. Dabria had gone inside to fetch some water, and then... nothing. She couldn't help but wonder- was this feeling of being crowded simply a side effect of her injury? How much more did she not remember from that fateful night? She found it difficult to put into words, this unfamiliar sensation that had taken over her body. She attempted to explain it to the doctors, her parents, and even Laura, but they all just looked at her with sympathy. No matter how hard she tried, she couldn't shake the feeling that she was no longer herself. She hoped that with time, the clouded and crowded feeling would dissipate. But sometimes she could hear a man's voice speaking to her from within her own mind, and it terrified her. He mostly offered advice on how to expedite her healing process - she couldn't help but wonder if it was her subconscious trying to communicate with her. But why would it take on the form of a male voice? It was all too weird, and so she tried to ignore it.

All she wanted was to see Laura and, of course, Dabria - even though he was still off limits according to her parents. Laura was her only visitor now that she was back home, she had visited Mia in the hospital multiple times while she was unconscious- but Mia had no recollection of these visits.

Her parents had confiscated her phone "for her own good," they claimed, but she knew it was really to prevent her from contacting Dabria. So Dabria sent messages through Laura, who acted as a messenger between them. And now, just a few days later, when Mia felt strong enough to go for a short walk, she made plans to meet up with him at his house - if they did it the next Sunday, he promised that his parents and the housekeepers, including the ever-present Calvin- would be out for the day at a new church opening, giving them privacy.

Meanwhile, Eddie and Alison were secretly tying up loose ends as they prepared to uproot their family and relocate to London. In light of the ever-present danger posed by the demonic Lord Nick, they had no choice but to flee for safety. Flights were already booked for the coming Thursday, and they hoped this fresh start would bring a sense of security and much-needed peace to their lives. However, there was one delicate matter they had yet to address: how to break the news to Mia. They knew she would not take kindly to leaving her friends and familiar surroundings, so they planned to tell her the night before they departed, giving her minimal time to process and potentially overreact to the sudden change in their plans. As they packed their suitcases with treasured belongings and important documents, their minds raced with both excitement and apprehension for what lay ahead in the bustling city of London.

On the Sunday before their planned departure, Mia managed to sneak away with Laura's help. They cleverly convinced Mia's parents that they were simply going for a leisurely stroll down to their favourite cafe for lunch and then spending some time at the beach. After much reluctance, Eddie and Alison agreed to let them go, unaware of Mia's true intentions.

As the afternoon wore on, Penny made her way over to check on Mia's recovery and spend some time with her friend, Alison. The two women were joined by Eddie on the deck, basking in the warm rays of sunshine while sipping on cups of freshly brewed coffee. As they chatted and caught up, the conversation turned to the new church that was opening in town.

Eddie and Alison shared a knowing look, and Alison revealed that some of her clients were eagerly anticipating the promised 'healings' at the church. They had specifically mentioned Lord Nick, adding he was known as Natas to his staff.

At the mention of this name, Penny's hands trembled, and she nearly dropped her cup. She couldn't keep it inside any longer - she had to tell Alison and Eddie what she had done- Through tears, she confessed about cloning Satan and creating Natas, changing her name, and burning down the science centre. The gravity of her actions finally sunk in for Penny as she saw the look of shock and horror on her friends' faces.

Eddie and Alison explained to Penny how Lord Nick had been responsible for the deaths of some of their friends and how he had been hunting them down from New York to Brighton -seeking revenge on Eddie. They recounted their entire story, from Eddies university days to present day. The three sat together, processing everything with a mix of disbelief and fear. But deep down, they all knew their tales were true and they were all in imminent danger.

With tears still streaming down her face, Penny apologized to Eddie and Alison for her foolish actions. They comforted her, assuring her that they would figure everything out together.

They sat on the deck, discussing their next steps, a sense of unease settled over them. It was nearing evening and there was no sign of Mia returning home yet.

THIRTEEN

L aura bid farewell to Mia at the entrance of Dabria's grand estate and continued her leisurely stroll up the esplanade towards the buzzing cafes on Jetty Road. Dabria had been eagerly awaiting their arrival on the front balcony, and upon seeing them, he bounded down the stairs to greet Mia. They embraced tightly in the doorway before Dabria led her inside and locked the door behind them.

"Would you like to sit inside or out on the balcony?" he asked, his dark eyes filled with adoration.

"Inside," Mia replied a little too quickly, still not fully recovered from her recent accident involving a balcony.

"Of course, silly me," Dabria chuckled, realizing his mistake. He knew it may be too traumatic for her and gently took her hand as they entered the plush living room. They settled onto a large, soft sofa facing each other, their eyes meeting in a loving gaze. Without a word, Dabria leaned in and pressed his lips to hers, their first kiss. It was gentle and tender, and Mia never wanted it to end.

They sank back into each other's arms, feeling completely content and lost in each other's presence. After some time passed, Dabria broke the enchanting spell with a suggestion:

"We should perhaps arrange for our parents to meet and see that we are all good people. Maybe then they'll allow us to be together."

"Have you told your parents about us?" Mia inquired softly.

Dabria's expression fell slightly, as he replied, "My father didn't say much - just smiled at me as if I were clueless. And my mother...well, she simply said that things have a way of working themselves out." His frustration was evident as he lamented their lack of support. "We're not children anymore - I'll be 17 soon and heading off to university next year. And you're already 17," he ranted fervently. Dabria tended to become animated when he felt strongly about something, and his passion for Mia was undeniable.

"Let's not worry about that right now," Mia said gently, pulling him back down onto the sofa beside her. They spent the rest of their day wrapped in each other's arms, stealing kisses and cuddles on the sofa. Dabria even made them some sandwiches and brought in cold bottles of coke for refreshment. As they snuggled together and watched a movie, Mia could feel the gentle strokes of Dabria's hand through her soft hair - a simple but powerful display of his love for her. And for that moment, nothing else mattered.

The movie had ended, but Mia and Dabria were lost in each other's company on the couch. As the credits rolled on the screen, they cuddled closer together. Suddenly, Mia froze as she heard approaching footsteps. She looked up to see Dabria's father standing in the doorway, a wierd look of pure glee on his face. Dabria quickly pulled himself into a sitting position and jumped up to introduce Mia to his dad, but Nicholas Green was already standing right in front of her.

"You must be Mia Sampson," he declared with a smug tone

Mia frowned slightly, "Mia Simpson," she corrected him, as she pulled herself up into a seated position. "Nice to meet you, Mr. Green."

"LORD Green," he responded firmly, correcting her.

"Oh Dad, it doesn't have to be so formal," Dabria interjected.

But his father didn't seem to hear him. He was almost salivating as he looked down at poor Mia. His normally deep voice had taken on an even deeper tone and for the first time in his life, Dabria felt scared of his own father. He reached out to help Mia off the sofa, but his father pushed him aside.

"Leave," he instructed Dabria sternly.

Dabria stood his ground, "No - Dad, what are you doing?"

"Now - leave," Nicholas Green's expression had turned cold and menacing. He was no longer Dabria's father; he was Natas now. And he would not let anyone take this prize away from him, no matter who was watching. Nick tried to calm Natas, not wanting his family to be caught up in his revenge, but Natas would not listen- he had waited long enough.

Shelley's heart pounded as she heard the commotion and came running, her feet slapping against the hardwood floors. She stopped in the doorway, her eyes widening in horror at the scene unfolding in front of her and her son. "What's going on, Nick?" she asked, but he didn't even acknowledge her presence.

Stepping further into the room, Shelley saw Mia looking terrified as she stared up at Nick like he was a monster. She could feel her own fear rising as she called out once more, "Nick, what is it?"

Finally turning to face her, Nick's eyes seemed to glow red as if possessed by some dark force. "She is mine!" he declared with a chilling certainty.

Shelley and Dabria stood frozen, their minds struggling to make sense of what was happening before them. Suddenly, Nick lunged forward and grabbed hold of Mia by her throat, lifting her off the sofa with ease. Her small frame dangled helplessly in front of his face as he held her tightly.

Mia's attempts to scream were stifled by Nick's grip, and an otherworldly voice escaped her lips instead. It was low and calm but sent shivers down everyone's spine. "This man is possessed by a devil," it declared, causing Nick to drop Mia to the ground.

As confusion reigned in the Green household, Shelley wondered what dark forces had taken hold of her beloved husband and how she could save him from their grasp.

Shelley's heart raced as she witnessed the terrifying events unfolding before her. She had never seen this side of Nick, this dark and malevolent presence that seemed to control him. As Mia lay gasping for air on the ground, a strange resonance filled the room, sending shivers down Shelley's spine.

Dabria, frozen in shock, looked from his father to Mia, his mind struggling to process the sudden turn of events. This was not the man he knew as his father; this was a sinister force wearing his face. "Dad, what's happening?" Dabria's voice trembled with fear and confusion.

Lord Nick stood tall and imposing, his eyes ablaze with an otherworldly intensity. A guttural sound emanated from deep within him as he turned to face Shelley, his expression twisted by a malevolent grin. "It's time for the reckoning," he growled in a voice that was not entirely his own. "I am Natas, the true Lord of this vessel," he proclaimed through Nick's lips, his eyes still glowing with an otherworldly light.

Shelley's fingers curled tightly around Dabria, the child she vowed to protect with her life. Her heart ached as she watched her husband, his once gentle and loving demeanour now twisted with darkness and evil. The memories of that fateful night all those years ago came flooding back when she had been violated. And now, as she stared at her husband, she wondered if he had been taken over by some malevolent force all those years ago, too. She clung to Dabria, trying to shield him from this horror and praying for a way to save her family from the grips of evil.

At that moment, Eddie, Alison, and Penny burst into the room, having figured out that Mia must have come to be with Dabria when they found out she was not with Laura. Lord Nick stood before them, his eyes glowing red.

"Welcome, Eddie Sampson, Alison Sampson, and Doctor Penelope MacDonald," he sneered. "How convenient to have you all here at once."

With a fierce growl, Eddie lunged towards Mia, his body poised to protect her from the looming danger. But Natas, with supernatural speed and strength, easily stopped him with one hand around his throat. Dabria screamed in terror, and he acted on pure instinct- Without hesitation, he freed himself from his mother's hold, grabbed an ice pick from the bar, and sprinted towards his father from behind. With a desperate thrust, he stabbed the weapon, aiming for the side of his neck; Natas turned and flicked his hand, and Dabria was sent flying; the ice pick clanged its way to the floor, and Dabria was slammed into the wall with a loud thud- He fell to the ground, unconscious. Shelley immediately ran over to her son, frantically trying to rouse him from his state.

"You have no idea the extent of my power," Natas roared, his voice echoing through the room. He reached over, grabbed the ice pick from the floor, and with a sinister smile he drove it into his own neck with force, piercing an artery and causing a gruesome spray of blood to drench the walls. Nick's legs gave out beneath him, he collapsed to his knees and then fell to the floor, landing in a pool of his own deep red blood.

His hand reached up and clutched at his neck, trying to staunch the flow of crimson liquid gurgling from his mouth and gaping throat. But it was no use, the blood rushed forth like a river breaking through a dam, consuming him and staining the once pristine floor beneath him. Every breath came out as a strangled gasp, as he fought for his last moments of life. And then it happened - Natas emerged from within him, revealing his true demonic form as he stepped out of Nicholas Green's body like a discarded shell. The air was thick with the metallic scent of blood and the sound of anguished cries filled the room as chaos ensued.

Natas gestured with his other hand, conjuring a vortex that would drag them all into the fiery depths of hell.

The dark figure of Satan stood at the base of the swirling vortex, his red eyes gleaming with anticipation as he eagerly awaited Natas's return. The boisterous sounds from above echoed down to him, and he assumed that his clone would bring favourable news. His twisted smile widened, revealing sharp teeth as he imagined the power and glory that awaited him once they were reunited.

The vortex swirled and roared, a relentless force that seemed to grow in intensity with every passing moment, a churning mass of fire and fury that threatened to pull everyone into its depths.

Mia, unknowingly protected by the angel's wings screamed in sheer horror and as the danger became more apparent, the angel unfurled its wings and revealed its true form, it doubled in size- towering over them in all its divine glory. Its once serene face contorted into a fierce visage, resembling a mighty serpent with razor-sharp fangs bared in a warning. The air crackled with energy and fear as they braced themselves against the impending battle.

He threw back his head and let out a blood-curdling scream that echoed through the room, to the heavens and beyond- preparing to battle against the encroaching darkness that threatened their very souls.

Everyone fell silent as the battle between light and darkness unfolded before them. Natas, the demonic entity, snarled and bared his fangs, but the angel that had resided with Mia stood his ground. His eyes blazed with determination, and the divine light shimmered around him, illuminating the room and casting eerie shadows.

The angel and the demon clashed in an epic struggle, their energies erupting and colliding with each other, shaking the very foundations of the house. The Sampsons, Penny, and Shelley watched in awe as the battle unfolded, knowing that their fate hung in the balance.

Shelley's knuckles turned white as she clung to Dabria, her body shook with fear and desperation.

The vortex, a swirling abyss of despair and chaos, gaped wide like the maw of some ancient, insatiable beast.

Natas's big hands clamped around Mia's delicate neck with an iron-like grip. Malevolent triumph sparked in his glowing red eyes as he stepped into the vortex, dragging her down with him deeper into the heart of hell itself. The heat from the fiery pits below licked at her skin, sending shivers of fear and dread through her body. Her screams echoed off the walls of jagged rock, mingling with the guttural laughter of demons lurking in the shadows. As they descended further, the air grew thick with the stench of sulphur and brimstone, a sickly sweet scent that made Mia's stomach churn. She could feel the weight of evil surrounding them, tightening its hold on her soul with every passing moment.

With forceful determination, he slammed her body to the ground and then quickly turned around, catching sight of the angel as it descended towards him.

The angel's wings beat against the oppressive darkness, each stroke a fading hope against the inevitable descent. His sword, once gleaming with divine radiance, now flickered dimly as shadows encroached upon its light. He landed amidst the scorched plains of the underworld, where the air reeked of sulphur and lament, and Satan awaited an unholy welcome for the winged soldier of the heavens.

The imposing figure of Satan loomed over the hellscape; his dark form twisted into a grandeur that oozed malevolence. Beside him stood Natas, the fiery hellscape stretched out before them, pulsating with otherworldly energy.

Satan's voice echoed through the abyss as he spoke, a sinister grin on his face. "Welcome," he said, thinking about how simple it would be for him and his clone to eliminate this angel together. The sounds of every fear that had ever haunted the night seemed to come together in a symphony around them.

The angel, undaunted by the dual horrors of Natas and his dark progenitor, stood firm and unyielding. He brandished his blade with defiance born from eons of celestial warfare, the light gleaming off its sharp edges like a beacon in the darkness.

In a fiery fury, Natas and Satan locked in battle against the angel, their movements fluid and precise as they attempted to strike down the angel who had dared to enter hell. The very fabric of the underworld seemed to tremble at their might, the ground cracking and shaking beneath them. It was a macabre dance, a deadly tango between three immortal beings bent on destruction. With each blow, their faces contorted in matching expressions of ferocity, mirroring each other's unrelenting resolve to emerge victorious.

Mia lay crumpled on the ground, her once vibrant form now still and lifeless. Demons encircled her, drawn to the scene of the fierce battle raging between Satan, Natas, and the angel. The air crackled with unearthly energy as the three powerful beings clashed, their weapons flashing and their roars echoing through the darkness. But then, as the angel's desperate cries for help echoed across realms, a sudden surge of divine power erupted from the void.

A burst of dazzling light brought forth an army of angels, their glorious forms shining with celestial wrath. With every movement, their divinity was magnified a hundredfold, dazzling against the horde of demonic creatures that cowered in their presence. It was a sight that was breathtakingly majestic and terrifyingly awe-inspiring at the same time.

Responding to the scream of the angel, hundreds of other angels descended upon hell through the portal that Natas had created. One of the celestial beings descended upon Mia, her form splayed out like a broken doll. Amid the chaos, the angel swooped in and lifted her into his arms, enfolding her in the shelter of his massive wings. Her soul and the soul of the Gnangkari were free as they followed close by, ascending towards the heavens. The angel transported her lifeless body through the swirling vortex and gently placed her near her family before returning to hell to continue battling against evil.

Eddie's hands moved frantically over his daughter's pale, lifeless body as he attempted to revive her with chest compressions and rescue breaths. His face was contorted in fear and desperation, his eyes darting between her face and his hands. Her soul hovered nearby as the Ngangkari soul drifted upwards towards heaven.

Satan's obsidian claws dug into the scorched Earth as he frantically scurried to aid his brother. The ground shook and trembled with their combined strength, causing plumes of dust and ash to rise into the air. The smell of sulphur and brimstone permeated the air as they clashed with the angelic forces, each side determined to emerge victorious in this epic showdown between light and darkness.

With every strike, sparks flew, and energy crackled, igniting the very air around them.

Rage consumed Satan as he stood, facing not one but two angels - a formidable challenge even for the Prince of Darkness. But he was not alone; his brother Natas fought with equal ferocity by his side, locked in battle against two more angels. In this crucial moment, their bond proved unbreakable.

The unexpected legion of angels caught the demons of hell off guard. For a fleeting moment, uncertainty flickered across Natas' twisted visage, an emotion as foreign to him as mercy. Satan roared as his demons recoiled, momentarily overcome by the sheer intensity of the heavenly host's powers. His deep, guttural roars filled the cavernous depths of hell, commanding his army to join in the ongoing battle against good.

But hell's forces were not easily cowed. Rallying beneath the banner of their dark lords, they surged forward with renewed malice. The battle that ensued was fierce, a cacophony of clashing steel and thunderous roars that echoed throughout the infernal domain.

Wings unfurled amidst flames, swords clashed with claws, and the ground ran crimson with an otherworldly ichor. Each angel fought with relentless fury, their strength unyielding, even as the demons matched them with equal fervour born from the depths of damnation.

Above the fray, the angel who had sparked this celestial onslaught battled on, his survival hanging by a thread yet uncut by despair. In the heart of hell, surrounded by untold malevolence, the fight for dominion over souls and salvation raged, a testament to the eternal struggle between light and dark.

The battlefield was a blur of motion, bodies collided, surrounded by the glimmering wings of angelic beings and the dark, leathery wings of demons, fire and light illuminated the chaotic scene.

The air was thick with the stench of burning flesh and singed feathers, a putrid mixture of sulphur and brimstone that seemed to permeate everything. As the battle raged on, the smell only grew stronger and more nauseating.

Eddie's screams of terror and desperation echoed through the air as he frantically tried to revive Mia. His hands shook as he checked her pulse, his heart pounded in his chest. Meanwhile, Alison and Penny stood helplessly by, unsure of how to assist in the dire situation. Shelley clung tightly to Dabria, tears streaming down her face as he lay unconscious on the ground.

The wind whipped at their clothes and hair, threatening to pull them away into the dark abyss below. Their hearts raced as they fought to stay grounded, the roar of the vortex and the war raging below drowned out all other sounds.

With a sudden burst of triumph, the victorious angels began their ascent from the depths of hell back into the realm of humanity. The once tumultuous vortex now lay silent, except for the faint rustle of thousands of radiant golden souls swirling around them. They moved with effortless grace, their glowing forms shimmering in the dimly lit room as they continued to rise toward the heavens. Their translucent bodies glowed with an otherworldly light that seemed to radiate from within. Slowly but surely, they returned to their human vessels, ready to resume their journey on Earth and fulfill their divine purpose.

The ground shuddered, leaving behind a gaping hole where the vortex once stood. In the midst of it all lay Lord Nick, his body motionless and his eyes closed in eternal slumber. The air was heavy with the scent of burnt ozone and the lingering aura of magic gone awry. The sight was haunting, a reminder of the immense power that had just been unleashed.

With a trembling hand, Penny finally managed to dial for help. In what felt like an eternity but was only minutes, ambulances, police cars, and fire trucks arrived on the scene. Mia's pulse was faint, her breaths shallow, as they carefully lifted her and Dabria into the waiting ambulance. Dabria stirred slightly; his eyes fluttered open as the vehicle sped off with sirens blaring.

The flashing lights of the emergency vehicles illuminated the shocked and frightened faces of those involved in this tragic incident. Eddie, Alison, Shelley, and Penny were left behind to recount the harrowing events to the authorities.

FOURTEEN

T he news spread like a raging wildfire, consuming the world in shock and disbelief. The once revered Lord Nick was dead, leaving behind a trail of shattered congregations who had placed their unwavering faith in his supposed 'healings'. But now, with his untimely demise, those supposed miracles had vanished into thin air, leaving behind a bitter sense of betrayal and confusion amongst his followers. The harsh reality of his deceiving ways came crashing down, shattering the illusion of salvation he had created.

The once bustling churches of The Church of Ancient Souls now sat desolate and abandoned, their once sacred spaces now eerie and haunting. Pews and altars remained untouched, gathering layers of dust and cobwebs as if time itself had stopped in this place. Some had even suffered a more dreadful fate, their scorched remnants serving as a grim reminder of the chaotic downfall that ensued when the truth about their deity was finally revealed.

Mia and Dabria cozied up on the couch, lucky to be alive.

For weeks, the story had dominated the news cycle, plastered on every screen and paper. And yet, they still couldn't resist the urge to watch it again and again. It was almost as if they couldn't believe it, even though they knew it truly happened. The images played out before them again, almost surreal in their clarity and detail. The shock and disbelief still lingered in the air, mingling with a sense of morbid curiosity that kept them glued to their screens. This was a moment that would be etched in history forever, a scene that no one could look away from despite its harrowing nature.

They were no longer forbidden from being together, and for that, they were grateful. Beside them, Eddie, Alison, Shelley and Penny sat in peaceful silence, safe from the danger that once threatened their lives.

With newfound determination and resilience, Shelley was determined to rebuild her life after finally discovering the truth about her husband's deceitful motives. She had already set the wheels into motion to get back into Law. The four adults had formed an unbreakable bond through their shared struggles, united in their bravery to confront the darkness that once loomed over them. Despite experiencing unfathomable terrors, they felt a strong sense of security as they sat together in each other's presence.

Mia and Dabria sat in silence, their eyes glued to the news report playing on the television screen. The bright moonlight filtered through the curtains, casting a faint glow on the quiet streets outside. It was as if the world was holding its breath after weathering a violent storm. In this newfound peace, Mia's mind drifted to the unknown and uncertain future that lay ahead. Despite her worries, she was determined to stay positive and focused on the present moment. Wrapped in Dabria's strong embrace, his warmth and comforting presence enveloped her like a shield of love. In that moment, Mia realized that she was not alone in this journey- She was surrounded by love and optimism for the future, and she was thankful for the potential for a better tomorrow, like a glimmer of sunlight peeking through the clouds after a turbulent storm.

She lay back and looked into Dabria's loving gaze, and for a brief moment, she thought she saw his eyes flash red…

For my Mumma who shines her bright light on me every day from the heavens.

For my wonderful Children and their partners, Christopher, Matthew, Crystal, Luke, Melissa, Ashlee, Ian, Kane, Jess and Seth.

For my fabulous siblings and their partners, Sandra, Jeff, Darren, Helen, Sheryl, Terri-ann, Kym, Eric and Toni.

For my amazing friends (in no particular order!) Paula and Rob, Naomi and Garry, Nola and Craig, Lynene and Ian, Jayne, Tania, Regan and Rob, Donna and Ian and Lynda and Ian.

Thankyou all for your support. I love and appreciate each and every one of you!

Thankyou to my publisher, Penguin – in particular, Lucas for all his wonderful help and guidance.

And of course; a HUGE thankyou to my readers- I really hope it was not one of those books where you get to the end and close it and say- well that was shit.

Through writing, I realised I only needed one person to believe in me and that person is me- and that I did and that I do. It took a while to silence the doubts and complete this novel, and if I had written it all those years ago when I started it – it would have been a very different story. To the naysayers - I say nay.

AUTHOR BIO

Lisa Diane O'Toole grew up in the Southeast of South Australia, in the quaint little country town of Penola and later moved to the big smoke- Adelaide where she is lucky enough to live near one of the beautiful beaches there. She is Mum to 5 wonderful adults, Foster Mum to a lovely teen, and Nana to 5 adorable children. She works full time in the Insurance industry but her passion is definitely in writing. Lisa spends her spare time walking her beautiful border-collie 'Leroy' on the beach, reading whenever she gets a spare moment and is an avid Steven King fan- she especially loves how his stories intertwine. She has a love/hate relationship with true crime shows and enjoys traveling the world via cruise ships. Lisa has been writing for many years- songs, poetry, and stories for all genres- this is her first published Novel.